BLACK POWDER

Also by Staton Rabin

Betsy and the Emperor
Margaret K. McElderry Books

Black POWDER

STATON RABIN

Margaret K. McElderry Books
New York London Toronto Sydney

Margaret K. McElderry Books
An imprint of Simon & Schuster Children's Publishing Division
1230 Avenue of the Americas, New York, New York 10020

Book design by Sonia Chaghatzbanian
The text for this book is set in Ehrhardt.
Manufactured in the United States of America
2 4 6 8 10 9 7 5 3 1

Library of Congress Cataloging-in-Publication Data
Rabin, Staton.
Black powder / Staton Rabin.—1st ed.
p. cm.
Summary: After his best friend is shot and killed, fourteen-year-old Langston borrows his science teacher's time machine and travels from Los Angeles in 2010 to Oxford, England, in 1278 to try to prevent Roger Bacon from publishing his formula for gunpowder.
ISBN-13: 978-0-689-86876-4
ISBN-10: 0-689-86876-6 (hardcover)
[1. Time travel—Fiction. 2. Bacon, Roger, 1214?–1294—Fiction. 3. Firearms—Fiction. 4. Gunpowder—Fiction. 5. Astronomy—Fiction. 6. Grief—Fiction. 7. African Americans—Fiction. 8. Los Angeles (Calif.)—Fiction. 9. Oxford (England)—History—Edward I, 1272–1307—Fiction. 10. Great Britain—History—Edward I, 1272–1307—Fiction.] I. Title: Black powder. II. Title.
PZ7.R1084Dr 2005
[Fic]—dc22
2004018311

The author and publisher wish to acknowledge the following for permission to reprint the copyrighted material listed below. Every effort has been made to locate all persons having any rights or interests in the material published here. Any existing rights not here acknowledged will, if the author or publisher is notified, be duly acknowledged in future editions of this book:

"Bring me all of your dreams" and "Hold fast to dreams," from *The Collected Poems of Langston Hughes,* by Langston Hughes, copyright © 1994 by the Estate of Langston Hughes. Used by permission of Alfred A. Knopf, a division of Random House, Inc., and Harold Ober Associates, Incorporated.

FIRST
EDITION

To Michael Lassaw, D.D.S., and his assistant, Michelle Casarella, two of the nicest people of this or any other millennium.

With thanks to my agents, Donna Bagdasarian and Lynn Pleshette, and my tour guides through time: Mark Polley, park ranger at Ford's Theatre; and my intrepid editor, Emma Dryden, who always has a compass.

Authors write many things and the people cling to them through arguments which they make without experiment, that are utterly false. . . . There are two ways of acquiring knowledge, one through reason, the other by experiment.

—*Roger Bacon, 1268*

If we could travel into the past, it's mind-boggling what would be possible. For one thing, history would become an experimental science, which it certainly isn't today. . . . We would be facing the deep paradoxes of interfering with the scheme of causality that has led to our own time and ourselves. I have no idea whether it's possible, but it's certainly worth exploring.

—*Dr. Carl Sagan, 1996*

BLACK POWDER

CHAPTER I

Oxford, England—January 1278

On any other morning the gnarled and veiny hands of Dr. Roger Bacon would have been carefully polishing a lens for the latest version of his own invention, the telescope. Or perhaps they would have been engaged in mixing smelly chemicals in long-necked glass bottles. Or even feeding the cat.

But on this particular morning Dr. Bacon was about to perform an experiment that would change the world forever—in ways so profound that even he could never have imagined them. And, in time, most would agree that his discovery hadn't changed the world for the better. In fact, very much the opposite.

But on this bright morning in Oxford, in the year 1278, Dr. Bacon was employed in what he was sure was good work. He poured measured amounts of yellow, black, and white powders into a heavy flour-filled sack that he'd dragged to one corner of the room. As an afterthought he added a bit more of the white powder. *Yes, a bit more, that should be just right,* Dr. Bacon mused, adding an extra pinch—as if he were the cook at Oxford University, where he ate (and complained loudly about) his afternoon meal each day.

Dr. Bacon tied the sack shut with a bit of string. Snuffing out a candle, he pinched off a small wad of the soft, warm tallow and molded it into two cone-shaped pieces. These he put in his ears.

After relighting the candle with a stick of wood from the fireplace, he used the candle flame to ignite a rope protruding from the flour sack. Then he walked across the room, sat on a stool—and waited.

Nothing happened.

Bitterly disappointed, Bacon crossed the room and kicked the sack in frustration. And just as he turned his back—

KABOOM!

The flour sack exploded. Flour rained down upon him, till he was coated with the stuff. Dr. Bacon now looked like one of the hapless, pumice-covered victims of the volcanic explosion in Pompeii, Italy, a millennium earlier. Or perhaps he looked more like a loaf of country bread—if loaves of bread were known to smile. Because the experiment had ended precisely the way Dr. Bacon had hoped. And, indeed, he was grinning from ear to ear.

Bacon danced a country jig. *Most inappropriate,* he thought briefly, *for a man of the Church.* But entirely appropriate, he decided, for a scientist who had just invented something of such great importance. And after so many failed attempts!

Outside Dr. Bacon's home young Niles had happened to be ambling by—counting the booty from his latest adventure as a pickpocket—when he heard the tremendous explosion. Niles dashed to the window of the doctor's home and looked in. There was Bacon, prancing about like a goat drunk on fermented grapes. *My gawd,* thought Niles, *the old bloke's gone barmy!*

"Dr. Bacon?" Niles called through the open window, wondering if perhaps it wasn't really the doctor after all. He stared, incredulous, at the powder-covered old man.

"I've done it, Niles!" Bacon shouted exultantly. "I've done it! I've made Greek fire!"

CHAPTER II

Neely Neubardt, a new member of the Tombs gang, stashed his pistol at his waist under his hooded sweatshirt as he walked jauntily down the alley. The metal felt cold against his bare skin, and a sharp wind cut his face like a razor. Neely had no particular mission tonight. He was just making his rounds—almost as the street cops did, in the parts of the neighborhood they weren't too scared to patrol. Neely practiced his swagger, moving fluidly to his own silent rhythm like he'd seen the older Tombs do.

Then, suddenly, he heard something hit the pavement. Loud and in a steady stream—like metal rain. Neely whipped around, gun drawn, hand trembling. Neely had never fired his gun before. And he secretly hoped he'd never have to.

Fortunately this time he didn't have to. The metal rain was made up of gun cartridges, but they were only empty ones, knocked from a fire escape by a clumsy cat.

"Pssst!" Neely said to the half-starved, mangy tom. "Whatcha doin'? Lookin' for girl kitties?" Neely put the gun back in his waistband.

The cat leaped to the ground, then wove its skinny body through Neely's ankles. It purred.

"Aw . . . ," Neely said, petting the animal's mottled coat. "Don't get all lovey-dovey on me. I ain't takin' you home. My mom'll kill me."

Suddenly Neely sprang upright at the sound of approaching footsteps. Terrified, he drew his gun.

It was a Vipers boy. *Couldn't be more than twelve,* Neely decided in a split second. It was clear the kid hadn't planned to run into one of the Tombs. *Hell, he's more scared than I am!* Neely thought. The kid was shaking, sweating, and reached for his own weapon only after he saw Neely had drawn his.

The two youths, one white and one black, stood just an arm's length apart, breathing hard, not saying anything. Not knowing how to get out of this mess.

"Don't shoot!" the black kid begged. "Please—I got a sister to take care of. We're orphans!"

Yeah, Neely thought. *And I'm a friggin' movie star.*

Before Neely could say anything, the kid dropped his gun and tore off down the alley like Roadrunner in the cartoons. All that was missing was the "Beep-beep!" and a cloud of dust.

Neely shrugged it off, picking up the discarded gun. The kid was a coward. *If all the Vipers are like that one, we Tombs got this whole neighborhood to ourselves!* Neely thought with a laugh.

As he walked away down the alley, Neely felt a sudden chill. He noticed his T-shirt was clinging to him, soaked with sweat. Suddenly it all didn't seem so funny.

CHAPTER III

The Vipers boy bolted into the empty school yard of Benjamin Banneker High, looking behind him every few steps. He hadn't stopped running for even a second since he'd fled the alley. Nervous, he chanced a look around. *I've lost him*, he thought with relief. *That was too damn close!*

The boy sat on a bench, trying to catch his breath. "Two, four, five, seven, nine, eleven . . ." He counted TV channel numbers in his head. That always helped him stay calm. " . . . Twenty-nine, thirty-three, fifty-four, sixty-three . . ."

"Wrong place, wrong colors, boy."

The Vipers boy looked up, but he'd already guessed what he'd see. Two teens—Tombs members—towered over him at both sides of the bench. He knew he was cooked.

A few minutes later the school yard was quiet again. The mangy cat from the alley had wandered onto the blacktop near the bench. Its gray paws were stained red by a puddle forming under the seat.

CHAPTER IV

At first glance no one would ever have predicted that Langston and Neely would end up as friends. They were as different as black and white—and, in fact, were.

Langston Davis was the kind of fourteen-year-old who would rather spend his evenings at home reading a Ray Bradbury book about Martians, or Dr. Kaku's latest essay on string theory, than pick up girls at a rave. His mother had a love for reading so passionate that she didn't care what Langston read, as long as it wasn't "those comic books with the girls that look like they're wearing metal brassieres" or "that porno junk on the Internet." Of course, even though science was all he cared about, she'd always hoped Langston would read poetry and stuff. After all, she'd even named him after a great African-American poet, Langston Hughes.

But the truth was, it wasn't just his mother's influence that accounted for Langston's bookishness. And it certainly wasn't his father's, an auto mechanic with an eighth-grade education who seemed to think books were just for propping up tire jacks. It was his science teacher's, Mrs. Centauri. Up until Langston started taking her ninth-grade astronomy course, "Secrets of the Cosmos," Langston had thought school was about as exciting as watching his basketball teammate "Gross-out" Gary Dunwoodie pick his nose. But Mrs. Centauri, who had the same name as a real star—one way out in outer space—changed all that. That woman had an imagination that made Langston feel the universe was a whole lot bigger than South-Central, and that his dreams could be even bigger than the universe.

As for Neely, it was hard sometimes to tell what kind of dreams he had—or if he even had any at all. His mother wasn't around much, and the guys he'd hung out with since his father took off last year . . . well, they seemed more interested in guns than gamma rays. But Neely and Langston had been friends since way back when they were rug rats—so long that Langston knew that Neely would get himself straightened out somehow, sooner or later. Neely was okay. He had helped Langston through some tough times, usually when his father was ragging on him again. "You give pretty good advice—for a white guy," Langston would tell Neely. They could still kid each other that way and not get mad.

"Io . . . Europa . . . Gany—oops! . . . Ganymede . . . Callisto . . ."

Neely shouted another name every time he managed to snatch the basketball away from Langston. Which, to tell the truth, was most of the time.

"Hey, that's Jupiter's moons!" Langston said, amazed. "Where'd you learn that?"

"Keep your mind on the game, dude. Amalthea . . . Metsit—"

"It's Metis," Langston corrected him, out of breath. "Not bad, for an amateur. Since when you interested in science?"

Neely turned around and swiped the ball from Langston again. He threw a one-hander, and it was nothing but net.

"See? I'm learning your game. Now if only you could learn mine," Neely crowed. "Twenty-four nothing. Keep this up and LeBron James himself will come here and arrest you for impersonating a basketball player."

Swoosh! Another slam dunk for Neely. Langston, mock-angry, tackled and wrestled him to the ground. But Neely got the upper hand and pinned Langston in a matter of seconds.

"You're spending too much time in that library, man." Neely grabbed his friend by the head. "Only place you got muscles is *here*."

"Hey! I'm getting stronger. Coach says he might even let me play in a game someday." Langston rolled up a sleeve and showed off a pretty good bicep. "I've been working out, man."

"Doin' what? Liftin' 'cyclopedias?"

Langston laughed. "No. Just my aspirations."

"Your aspi-what?"

"Never mind. It's not just about sports," he said, taking the ball from Neely. "You wouldn't understand, basketball boy." Langston was only kidding about the insult, and Neely knew it, playing along.

"Oh, yeah? Think I don't know nothing? Want to hear me say the rest of Jupiter's moons?"

"Man, Neely, if you got a memory like that, what're you doing cutting classes?"

"Got more important things to do."

Langston sat down on the curb, looking more serious. "Yeah. Sure. I know."

"You're not going to start on me again," Neely warned. It was dark now, and the automatic lights on the basketball court were coming on.

"You're running with the wrong crowd," Langston said, sounding more like his mother than he wanted to.

"There he goes! Just like the Energizer Bunny. Keeps goin' and goin'!"

"I'm serious, man. Don't you got anything you want to do with yourself? Don't you want to be something? Here . . ."

Langston spun the ball like a planet and tossed it to Neely.

"Jupiter. Don't you ever wonder what it'd be like to go up there?" Langston looked up at the darkening sky and pointed to the horizon. A few bright pinpricks of light were already appearing against the blackness, near the curve of the earth. Langston grew quiet. When he spoke again, he sounded like he'd fallen under some sort of spell. "Comets and supernovas . . . ice that's hot like a stove. And seas made of silver mercury." He turned back to face Neely. "Don't you ever dream about . . . anything?"

Neely tossed the ball back—too hard.

"Not everybody's lucky like you, Lang. You got a family, man. Well, my boys in the gang? They're mine."

Langston glanced at a newspaper that was lying flat on the ground. He tucked the basketball in the crook of his arm, picked up the paper, and shoved it into Neely's hand.

"This what your 'family' does for kicks, Neely? Smoke babies?"

Neely looked at the photo under the newspaper head-line. It was of the Vipers boy he'd encountered in the alley the night before. Only, this picture must have been his school portrait; he was smiling, with hair slicked down like his mama had done it for him—looking like any other little kid you'd see in the lunchroom. The headline read, 12-YEAR-OLD GUNNED DOWN BY GANG MEMBERS.

"I . . . I had nothing to do with this, man. I swear!" Neely said. And even though he hadn't, his hands shook as he held the paper. He wondered if Langston would believe him. *Does he know me good enough to know I'd never shoot anybody?* Neely wondered. *At least, not if it really came down to it. Not even to stay in the Tombs?*

Langston only said, "Right." And it was clear he didn't really believe his friend.

Langston threw the basketball down at Neely's feet. He tramped back up the stairs of the projects to his apartment, leaving Neely behind.

CHAPTER V

Langston stood shivering on the dark roof of his apartment building, peering through a four-and-a-quarter-inch reflecting telescope. His mother had bought it for him secondhand for Christmas last month, but it worked as good as new.

A red-gold crescent moon—like a giant coin with a big bite taken out of it—hung over the city, and that's what he was focusing on. Every few minutes Langston had to rub the telescope eyepiece with a special cloth, since it was so unusually cold out that his breath made fog on the lens.

Langston's mother sat in a chair next to him, flexing her arthritic knees to keep them from locking in position. She didn't usually look through the telescope. Mostly she was just there to keep her son company.

The trapdoor in the roof rose up, and somebody poked his head through the opening.

"All right, you want to get frozen like Mrs. Paul's fish

sticks, you folks go right ahead and stay out here in the cold. See if I mind."

"Only a few more minutes, Dad," Langston said, daring to defy his father. "I gotta show Mama the moon."

"Yeah, I once told your mama I'd give her the moon too, and look where that got us."

Langston's mother smiled. She was used to her husband's ways, understood him, and didn't mind his moods. Langston's father grumbled, ducked his head back down, and pulled the trapdoor shut behind him. Langston always breathed a little easier when his father wasn't around.

"Come take a look, Ma," Langston said, making some final adjustments to the Barlow lens.

His mother didn't make a move, but grimaced, as if even thinking about getting up made her knees hurt.

"Come on. The moon'll move soon," Langston urged.

"It's been here a whole lot longer than me. You'd think that moon man'd get some cricks in his joints by now."

But Langston's mother got up from the chair and lumbered over to her son.

"Your eyes used to the dark yet?" Langston asked. "Here, take a look. And don't breathe on the lens. You'll fog it up."

She gave him a sassy look. "Well, excuse me for living, Mr. Wizard."

Langston's mother peered through the eyepiece. She saw the big moon craters looking clear as day. Almost the way they looked in the photographs those astronauts had taken on the moon when she was young. But Langston's mother wasn't the sort to let her emotions hang out for everybody to see, like laundry on a clothesline.

"Well," she said.

"Isn't that something?"

"Well. The same moon the great Booker T. Washington saw. The same one Benjamin Banneker saw. Well."

"Something, huh?"

Suddenly the smile melted from his mother's face.

"It's got blood on it," she said.

"Huh?"

"That's what they said the night Abe Lincoln got shot. 'Blood on the moon.' It looked red, just like it does now."

"That's not blood," Langston explained. "That's just the atmosphere we're seeing it through. Like a sunset. Mrs. Centauri told me."

But his mother still seemed uneasy.

She walked to the trapdoor leading downstairs and opened it.

"Your father's waiting on me," she said. Langston reached out to give her a hand as she stepped down into the passageway. She turned back to look at him. "Not too long," she admonished. "And take out the kitchen trash before bed. Third time I've had to ask you today."

Langston nodded.

After his mother left, Langston made some adjustments to the equatorial mount and aimed his scope at Mars. While reaching for a new lens, he bumped into the telescope, shifting its focus from Mars down to the street.

"Damn!" He'd have to adjust the settings all over again.

But for a moment he became interested in what he was seeing through the lens: the streets of South-Central, blocks and blocks away. He'd never looked at his own neighbors through the telescope before. Maybe because that would have felt wrong—like he was spying on them. But it wouldn't hurt to look just this once. . . .

Then, to his amazement, Langston saw someone he recognized. It was Neely! He was standing on a corner talking to his gang leader. No, not talking—arguing. That was clear from the way their arms were waving and their mouths were twisting in anger as they spoke.

Langston adjusted the telescope lens for a closer look. Neely was holding a newspaper, pointing angrily to the photo of the murdered Vipers kid. He seemed to be telling off his gang leader. Then he ripped off his colors—his bandanna, which identified him as a member of the Tombs—and threw it to the ground. Neely turned his back on the gang leader and started to leave.

"Way to go, Neely!" Langston said aloud, pumping his fist in the air. "I knew you could do it, man!"

Langston swiveled the telescope on its mount and followed Neely with it as his friend walked down the street. Suddenly Neely dropped out of view. Puzzled, Langston trained the telescope back on the gang leader. The guy was standing there with a gun in his hand, and then he turned and scaled a fence, dropping the gun as he climbed. A terrible chill ran down Langston's spine. And all at once he knew with a terrible certainty what must have happened.

Without stopping to think, Langston wrenched open the trapdoor and took the stairs down two at a time. He passed his father on the stairwell.

"Whoa, boy! Where do you think . . ."

But Langston didn't stop. He flew out the front door of the building.

He covered ten blocks in only a few hundred beats of his heart. And he found just what he feared he would.

Neely was lying on his back in the gutter. His breathing was labored, and he was bleeding from a neck wound. Frantic, Langston tried to cover the hole with his Anaheim Angels jacket.

"I'm here. It's Langston. Hang on, Neely! You hear?"

There was the flicker of a response on Neely's face. He mumbled something Langston couldn't understand.

"Damn!" Langston said to himself. "I should've called an ambulance."

He looked over his shoulder, hoping to see a pay phone, a store open—anything. But all he saw was a white cabbie driving by at a slow roll. Langston ran toward the taxicab.

"Hey! Please stop! My friend's been—"

But the cabbie locked all the car doors.

"No—you don't understand!" Langston shouted through the window glass. "I—we need help, man! Get on your cell! Call 911!"

But the cabbie floored his accelerator and the car screeched away.

Langston ran back to Neely's side. His friend's breathing had stopped. Langston tried desperately to remember how to do CPR.

"Clear the airway, clear the airway. Jesus—what's next? Chest compressions. That's right! But how many seconds between breaths? God, I don't remember!"

Whatever Langston was doing, it seemed to help. Neely was breathing again.

"Lang?" Neely whispered.

"We're going to Jupiter together, man," Langston said, hoping to keep his friend talking. "Remember? You and me."

"Hot ice . . . and silver mercury." Neely started to shake violently. Langston ripped off his sweater and laid it over Neely's chest.

"That's right. Stick around, okay? Neely?"

"O-okay," Neely said. Langston could barely hear him now. He leaned closer. Neely was fading fast.

"Who popped me? I don't re—"

"Shhh . . . never mind. Hang on, man. I'm gonna get help. I promise—I'll be back," he told Neely. "Just hang on!"

As Langston stood up to go, Neely grabbed his sleeve.

"Lang," he said weakly. "Didn't smoke that kid. Last night. I'd never—"

"I know," Langston said truthfully. "I never really thought you did."

Neely still didn't let go of Langston's sleeve. He had a desperate look in his eyes. His grip was vise tight—as if it took all the strength he had left in him.

"Didn't smoke that kid." He tried to sit up, but Langston gently pushed him back down.

Neely shuddered. His grip on Langston's sleeve slackened.

"Seas of silver mercury . . . ," he said, a smile forming on his deathly pale face. "Beautiful."

Neely let out a heavy sigh. His chest rose and fell for the last time.

Langston folded in two, screaming.

CHAPTER VI

Neely's funeral mostly had people Langston didn't even know. The police had finally located Neely's father and given him the terrible news about his son. But Neely's old man was too drunk to show up for the funeral. Neely's mother stayed away too. She'd gone half crazy with crying and blaming herself for what had happened to her son, so they put her under some kind of sedation. The Banneker High School principal came to the cemetery. Langston had to give the guy credit for that. And Langston and his parents were there, of course, and Mrs. Centauri. But most of Neely's so-called friends were afraid to go to the funeral—afraid the Tombs would hear about it and pop them, too.

As they all stood by the grave site, the reverend said a few boring but respectful things about Neely, whom he'd clearly never met. He spoke about the tragedy of dying young and even threw in something about the evil of guns, "which have cruelly taken so many of our brothers from us before their time." Langston half listened as the reverend droned on, but was too numb to feel much of anything.

Langston's father studied his son out of the corner of his eye and felt a strong impulse to put an arm around his shoulders. But he couldn't quite bring himself to do it, even though his heart was breaking for him. He thought it would weaken the boy to have his father's comfort at a time like this. Life was tough—it was time his son learned it. He'd have to sooner or later. And being coddled by his father would just slow it all down.

Langston, of course, had no idea his father was thinking about any of this. He just glanced over and saw his father standing there staring at the ground, seeming not to care at all about him or what had happened to Neely. Same old, same old.

Just before they lowered Neely's coffin into the ground, Langston placed a photo of the planet Jupiter on it. Then he stood there—almost at attention—while the burying business got done.

As the final shovelful of dirt covered Neely's coffin, Langston felt a steady, comforting hand on his shoulder. It was his mother's.

CHAPTER VII

That Thursday at school Langston found an intriguing note taped to his locker. Scribbled on the back of a topographical map, the note invited him to a place he'd never been before.

Since Neely's death Langston hadn't felt like doing much of anything; still, he was too curious about this invitation to turn it down. He knew his mother would throw a fit if she knew the truth, so he told her he was going to the planetarium that evening to work on a science project for class, and hitched a ride to his real destination. After all, Langston thought, it was a long way up to Mrs. Centauri's home in the mountains around L.A., and he had no other way to get there. What was he supposed to do? Say "Dad, do you mind driving me up to the San Gabriels so I can visit that crazy science teacher of mine you hate so much?" Sure. That would go over real good.

The guy who picked him up said that he didn't mind giving him a lift, that lots of people had done the same thing for him back when he was a young wild thing, and he was headed up that way anyway. The driver of the psychedelic orange-and-green milk truck looked like one of those hippies from back in the 1960s. He had long, ratty-looking gray hair in a ponytail, a tie-dyed T-shirt, and a few strands of heavy beads around his neck. But at the same time, the guy was wearing a white milkman's uniform and hat. He bobbed his head along to the beat of a Rolling Stones song playing on the radio.

"'I can't GIT NO!'" the driver sang along, pounding the steering wheel. "'Satis-FAC-shun!'"

The name printed on the outside of the truck was STRAWBERRY FIELDS FARMS—like the title of the song by the Beatles. To Langston, the whole idea of delivering glass milk bottles in a truck seemed like something out of a really old movie.

"Why you traipsing all the way up here, man?" the driver asked him as they bumped along on the road. The truck probably hadn't had its shocks replaced since 1968.

"My science teacher invited me. She wants to show me something," Langston said, his teeth rattling with every bump.

The hippie took one hand off the wheel, nudged Langston in the ribs, and laughed.

"Show you something, huh? Far out, man! I had a lady, Mrs. Asher, for science when I was a kid. She wore white boots and miniskirts—hoo-WEE!"

What I wouldn'ta given to do a few 'experiments' with her!"

"No," Langston said, feeling embarrassed, "it's nothing like that. She just wants to show me something through her telescope tonight."

"Yeah, you just stick to your story, man. 'I can't GIT NO! Satis-fac-SHUN!'"

The hippie turned down the radio. "I'm getting too wired, man. It happens sometimes." He made a faint humming noise for a while, sounding like, "Oooommmm . . ." The hippie seemed to go into some sort of trance. Langston wasn't sure this was such a good thing to do on these narrow, winding mountain roads. The driver's eyes fluttered and his head started nodding slowly toward the steering wheel.

The truck was headed straight for the steel barricades on the edge of the cliff.

"Look out!" Langston yelled. He reached over, grabbed the steering wheel, and turned it—just in time. The truck swerved and swayed wildly, making the milk bottles in the back clink loudly against one another.

"Sorry, man," the hippie said. "Guess I got too mellow for a moment there."

They drove the rest of the way in silence. But Langston kept a keen eye on the hippie to make sure he didn't nod off again.

Finally, to Langston's enormous relief, they came to a stop near a big house at the top of the mountain.

Mrs. Centauri's home was like nothing Langston had ever seen. It looked more like an astronomical observatory than somebody's house. It was made of smooth red stone, like a giant laboratory, and it had a big dome on one part of it, like an upside-down cereal bowl.

While Langston hopped out onto the sidewalk, the hippie went around to the back of the truck and took out a small wire cage filled with milk bottles. He walked to the front door of the house and opened a metal box on the doorstep. He referred to a clipboard he was carrying, then counted out three bottles, put them in the box, and closed the lid.

"That'll do it," he said.

"You deliver all the way up here?" Langston asked.

"You got some problem with that?"

Langston shrugged. "Well, this looks like the place. Thanks a lot . . . er . . . man."

"Give me five," the hippie said. Langston was confused for a moment and just stared at the man's outstretched hand. Then he remembered something he'd seen on an old TV rerun, and slapped the guy's hand with all his might.

The hippie smiled and got back in his truck.

"Not so hard next time!" he called out, waving, then drove away. "'I can't GIT NO! . . .'"

CHAPTER VIII

The door knocker looked like some sort of flying monster—like a creature from a medieval church or castle in a storybook. Griffins, or gargoyles, Langston thought they were called. Mrs. Centauri had a strange sense of humor, so he wasn't too surprised. He lifted the metal ring and knocked on the door.

There was no answer. He knocked again. What would he do if he'd come all this way and Mrs. Centauri wasn't home? Still no answer. He grabbed the doorknob. To Langston's astonishment, it almost seemed to turn by itself, and the door swung open.

"Mrs. Centauri? Mrs. C.?" he called, walking in cautiously. The place seemed deserted.

"Woof!"

A big rottweiler stood just a few feet away, fangs bared, growling at him.

Langston froze, not sure what to do next. He'd once

read that if you ran into a bear in the woods, you should play dead. But he doubted this dog was dumb enough to be fooled by that. And by the looks of this one, if Langston played dead, the dog might just eat him.

A girl of about six suddenly wandered into the room like she'd been expecting him, carrying what Langston recognized as an astrolabe—an ancient sort of compass for finding things in the night sky.

"Oh, don't mind Sirius," she said. "He's not real."

The dog crouched and continued to snarl.

"He looks pretty real to me," Langston said.

The girl just ignored him, sat down cross-legged on the floor, and started to play with the astrolabe. The dog left her alone. *This has to be Mrs. Centauri's kid,* Langston thought. What other kid that young would be playing with a complicated scientific instrument?

Since the dog didn't seem to be coming any closer, Langston chanced looking around. Everywhere he looked were high-tech computer consoles with bright colored lights and strings of data—mathematical equations and declinations of celestial bodies—strewn across their screens. Giant blow-up photos of nebulae and 3-D models of planets hung from the ceiling. Framed portraits of famous physicists and astronomers from the past to the present covered every wall: Galileo, Copernicus, Einstein, even Carl Sagan and Michio Kaku—as well as a few other guys that Langston didn't recognize. One of them had a long, hawkish nose and wore a brown, hooded cloak—like a monk.

The girl started talking to him, but Langston was more interested in the room than what the kid had to say.

"I'm Alpha. Like the star. I'm going to *be* a star."

"Alpha . . . Centauri," Langston said, putting it together.

"My dad wanted to name me Tiffany or Heather. But Mom didn't go for it. She was afraid I might grow up to work in a tanning salon or something."

"Uh-huh." Langston was barely listening. He pressed a red button on the wall near a model of Saturn. Suddenly all the moons and rings were set in motion around his head.

"Mom picked Alpha," the girl continued. "She says stars in the sky stay the same for a zillion zillion years. And then they die. *Kaboom!* Like Kelli Pallazo's poodle that ate drain cleaner."

"Huh? That's too bad."

Langston ducked a moon of Saturn as it swung by his head.

"You're Mom's smarty-brain student, aren't you? She told me not to call you that."

Langston nodded, embarrassed. "Well, I don't know if I'm—"

"Mom thought Alpha Centauri would be funny. I

mean, not like TV funny. Weird funny. You better not laugh, or I'll pull out your eyelashes!"

"Hmm? No, I won't. It's a nice name. Is your mom around?"

Alpha pointed toward a corner of the room. Mrs. Centauri was engrossed in studying a star chart. Langston approached and tapped Mrs. Centauri on the shoulder.

Mrs. Centauri jumped. "Langston! Welcome to my little mountain abode. Pretty wild, huh?"

He pointed to the star chart. "What are you looking at?"

"G78.2 plus 2.1, DR4, a gamma Cygni supernova remnant. A type S with a spectral index of 0.5. Can you tell me the ascension and declination?"

Langston knew that Mrs. Centauri was testing him, and he liked that she thought he was smart enough to figure it out. He studied the map, looking for the coordinates.

"Umm . . . right ascension twenty, twenty, forty. No, that's twenty, twenty, *fifty*. Declination . . . plus forty, twenty-six."

"Bingo! Give that man twenty golden doohickeys!"

Mrs. Centauri smiled at him and winked. When he didn't smile back, she looked concerned, her eyes radiating compassion.

"Sorry I didn't have much time to talk with you the past few days. How're you doing, kiddo?"

Langston shrugged.

"Did they catch the creep who did it?"

Langston nodded. "I picked him out in the police lineup the other day."

Langston felt awkward talking about Neely. He tried to change the subject, pointing toward the creature that was still growling at him near the door. "I didn't know you had a dog."

"I don't." Mrs. Centauri pressed a button on her desk and the dog vanished.

CHAPTER IX

"Kowabunga!" Langston was flabbergasted.

"He's a hologram," Mrs. Centauri explained. "My home security system."

She pressed the button again and the dog reappeared, looking as real and ferocious as ever.

Alpha tugged at her mother's sleeve.

"Mom, it's six o'clock. Sirius is hungry."

"Okay," she replied. "Go ahead."

Alpha poured some dog food into a metal bowl. She set it on the floor next to Sirius. Langston thought the whole thing was pretty silly. But a moment later the dog was eating the food! Now Langston was really confused.

"Hey! I thought you said he's just a—"

"Langston," Mrs. Centauri interrupted. "Can I trust you to keep a secret? No, I shouldn't have said that. I know I can."

Langston nodded.

"Come here, Sirius. Be a good boy. Come here." Sirius immediately stopped gorging himself and trotted eagerly over to Mrs. Centauri.

"Pet him," she said to Langston. "Go ahead."

Langston slowly reached out to touch the dog.

"He's solid!" Langston cried. "I can feel him."

Sirius nipped him.

"Ow!"

"Sorry," Mrs. Centauri said, examining Langston's hand. The skin wasn't broken.

Mrs. Centauri whistled. Another dog, identical to Sirius but much more passive and unresponsive, waddled into the room.

"Is that his brother?" Langston asked.

"That's Sirius too. Or Sirius One, actually. Two parts of the same dog."

"Like twins?"

"Like one dog," she explained, "with his feelings and thoughts in a separate body. They're in the hologram, Sirius Two," she said, pointing to the lively dog that had been eating a moment before. Then she indicated the passive, dopey dog. "And—well, there's nothing but an empty shell left in poor Sirius One here."

Alpha walked stiffly, as if she was imitating a character in an old horror movie. "He's like the Zombie!" she said.

"But don't worry," Mrs. Centauri added, "it doesn't hurt the dog. It's only temporary."

"Yeah," Alpha said. "Mom knows how to glue him back together again."

Langston looked back and forth between the two dogs as Alpha tried to feed Sirius 1 his dinner. Sirius 1 lolled lazily on the floor, uninterested in the food. Langston shook his head.

"One dog. How do you *do* this?"

From her desk Mrs. Centauri lifted a rectangular box that looked like the laser machines Langston had seen at school. She opened a back panel and removed a blindingly bright silver crystal from it.

"This is an iridium crystal," Mrs. Centauri said, handing it to Langston. "Iridium's a rare element on Earth. But it's common in asteroids. I found this beauty in that big asteroid crater in Arizona."

"Mom went to Arizona, and all I got is this lousy T-shirt!" Alpha said, tugging at her clothes.

Mrs. Centauri shushed her and continued. "Ordinary holograms—like those ghosts you see dancing around the haunted house at Disneyland?—are created using ruby lasers. But when I make a hologram of a living thing using an iridium laser, something really . . . weird happens."

Alpha pointed to the dogs. "Thing One and Thing Two!"

"Cool!" Langston said. "Have you tried it on a person?"

"You remember seeing me at school last Thursday?" Mrs. Centauri asked.

"Thursday? Of course."

"Well, that wasn't me. Not exactly, anyway."

"Oh. Cool," Langston said again, though with slightly less enthusiasm. It was certainly interesting, but the whole thing was so weird it made Langston feel a little uneasy.

Mrs. Centauri led him into another room—the one with the big dome over it. There was a giant reflecting telescope under the dome. It was the biggest telescope Langston had ever seen—with a mirror that must have been sixty inches in diameter! Mrs. Centauri pulled a lever located high atop a bookcase, and there was a loud rumbling and scraping sound. The floor shook a little. Mrs. Centauri pointed to the dome and Langston looked up. He could already see a patch of starry sky through it. The dome was retracting, opening the whole ceiling to the night sky!

Mrs. Centauri pressed a key on the giant telescope's computerized control panel that rotated the instrument a few degrees on some sort of mount. The telescope came to a stop, and she peered into the eyepiece.

"It's supernova 1987A," Mrs. Centauri said. "Want a look?"

Langston climbed up a couple of stairs and looked

through the eyepiece. He saw the beautiful remnants of a dying star.

"Hmmm . . . that's that supernova that exploded in the Large Magellanic Cloud in 1987," he said.

Alpha hopped into the room to join them. "Mom went there last week."

"What?" Langston croaked.

Alpha's hand flew to cover her mouth. "Oopsie," she mumbled. "I wasn't supposed to tell."

"It's all right, Al," Mrs. Centauri said, patting her daughter's shoulder. "I was going to tell him anyway. By making holograms that contain all of a person's thoughts and abilities, I can send them out like astronauts into space—on a beam of laser light. Anywhere in the universe. As far away as you can dream! Without a spaceship."

This was really getting too weird.

"You're kidding. Uh . . . right?" Langston asked.

Mrs. Centauri focused on his eyes like a laser beam.

"Flight one forty-seven, leaving for Pittsburgh, Houston, and the constellation Orion," she said. "Now boarding at gate three. . . ."

Mrs. Centauri stopped talking, a question in her eyes.

"You *are* kidding. Aren't you?" Langston asked again, his voice a little shaky.

Mrs. Centauri and Alpha both shook their heads at the same time.

So they were serious. And all at once Langston understood that Mrs. Centauri had just made him a real offer. An utterly amazing offer. One that nobody had ever gotten before.

He had to think about his answer for only a second.

"If I go, you'll get me back here okay? I mean, like, I have a math test tomorrow."

Mrs. Centauri grinned and slapped him on the back. "I knew I could count on you, kiddo!"

CHAPTER X

Langston stood in a circle marked on the living-room floor. Mrs. Centauri nudged him a little to position him so he'd be standing right on the X at the circle's center. There was a hum as she turned on the laser. Langston held his breath nervously. Then the humming noise stopped.

"That's it," Mrs. Centauri said. "You're done."

Langston didn't feel any different. And he was still standing right where he had been.

"But nothing happened," he said.

"Is that so?" Mrs. Centauri said, hands on her hips. "Look behind you."

Langston turned around and gasped. Sitting lazily on the sofa was his identical twin. He looked exactly like Langston, only his eyes were kind of vacant and he had a goofy smile on his face. Like he didn't know anything or like somebody on drugs. Langston felt his own body all over, to make sure everything was still there.

"That's your shell," Mrs. Centauri explained.

"What happens to him when I go . . . away?"

"Don't worry," she replied. "He's too passive to cause any trouble."

"I don't know, Mom," Alpha said with a warning tone in her voice. "That one of you that you left behind last week got pretty hairy. She—"

Mrs. Centauri waved her hand to silence her daughter. She began leafing through the pages of a big book called *Almanac of Asteroid Orbital Positions, 1200–2050*. She looked up and turned to Langston.

"We'll send you . . . what? . . . say, about a hundred forty-five light-years into space?"

"Sounds good to me," Langston said, swallowing hard.

"That's the distance light can travel in one hundred forty-five years," Mrs. Centauri said. "The sunlight that bounced off Earth a hundred forty-five years ago has been traveling out into space ever since, carrying images of the way things looked on Earth at the time. If you chase those light beams into deep space and catch up with them, you can look back toward Earth and see it as it was a hundred forty-five years ago—in 1865. Near the end of the Civil War. Pretty cool, huh?"

"Near the . . . you . . . you mean like Gettysburg? And slaves and picking cotton? *That* Civil War?"

Alpha started marching around the room like a soldier, singing loudly, "Gory, gory hello-lou-ya! Gory, gory hello-lou-ya!"

"You see," Mrs. Centauri explained to Langston, "looking at stars or planets in space from very far away is really like traveling back in time." She turned briefly to give Alpha a sharp look. "Cool it, Private Centauri. At ease." Alpha stopped singing, and Mrs. Centauri turned back to Langston. "So the farther away from Earth you get, the further back in Earth's time you can see. It's almost like watching an old movie! Here." She handed Langston a small telescope. "You'll need this to get a close view of Earth from out there. It's got more power than telescopes a hundred times its size."

"Thanks," Langston said. He peered into the eyepiece and looked out through the window with it at the sky.

"Yow!" he said, jumping. A huge, hairy monster with fangs and big, glittery eyes filled his telescope view. "Man, it's like a *Star Wars* alien invasion out there!"

"Chill out, whiz kid," Mrs. Centauri said, taking the scope from him to look through it. "That's just *Musca domestica*."

"Holy moly! What planet does *that* come from?"

"*Earth*, Captain Lamebrain," said Alpha.

"Alpha! That's not nice," Mrs. Centauri scolded. To Langston she said, "That's a common housefly you're seeing—*Musca domestica*—and it's a normal-size one. It's probably thousands of miles away."

Langston breathed a sigh of relief and let out a long,

low whistle. "Jeez! You weren't kidding when you said this scope was strong."

Mrs. Centauri handed the telescope back to him and studied her asteroid map and tables some more. While Langston checked out the telescope, Alpha started playing with a toy gun, running around saying, "Kapow!" and pretending to shoot at the dogs. She fired a pretend shot at Langston.

"Boom! You're dead!" Alpha shouted. Langston flinched.

"Alpha!" Mrs. Centauri yelled, snatching the toy from her daughter. "Where did you get that? You know I don't want you playing with guns. Even toy guns."

Mrs. Centauri looked at Langston. "I'm so sorry," she said.

He just shrugged and said he was fine. But he wasn't, not really.

Mrs. Centauri returned to the table and picked up her asteroid map. She studied it intently as she led the way back into the observatory.

"Normally," she said, "it would take you one hundred forty-five years to get out that far on a laser beam. But I'm going to bounce you off some asteroids to boost your speed beyond the speed of light. Their orbits are in just the right configuration now to do that. Only happens for eight days every eight hundred eighty-eight years. This is your lucky day, Langston!"

CHAPTER XI

"Homework time, Al." Mrs. Centauri gave her daughter a little pat on the behind, nudging her out the door. "Time to skedaddle."

"Aw, Mom. You always make me miss the good parts!"

Mrs. Centauri gave her a warning look, and Alpha shuffled reluctantly down the hall.

As soon as Alpha had gone, Mrs. Centauri pushed a button hidden under a Chinese vase.

"Stand back," she told Langston.

Langston watched as the giant telescope started sinking slowly down into the floor. Finally the whole thing had lowered into the basement. A wooden panel made a whooshing noise, covering the hole in the floor where the telescope had been.

Mrs. Centauri pointed to the center of the wooden panel. "That's your cue, kiddo. Find your mark."

Langston stood in the spot under the open dome. He craned his neck so he could get a look at the computer screen Mrs. Centauri was working on. It was the monitor of a computer panel that operated a giant laser. The computer screen asked, *"Today's date?"* Mrs. Centauri typed in, *"January 14, 2010."*

"Distance in light-years to destination?"

She typed in, *"144.75."*

"Coordinates?"

Then she programmed into the computer the exact location of Langston's destination, Washington, D.C.: latitude 38°53′N, longitude 77°2′W.

The computer monitor flashed the results: *"Earth view: District of Columbia, U.S.A., April 14, 1865."*

Mrs. Centauri pressed a button marked POWER ON. There was a humming sound.

"We're all set," said Mrs. Centauri. "Since you're a hologram, you can survive anywhere—even in space without oxygen. And the heat from the laser won't hurt you. It'll just carry you gently into space."

Langston trusted Mrs. Centauri. Still, this wasn't like any of the experiments they had done in "Secrets of the Cosmos." If something went wrong here, it wasn't like the worst thing that could happen would be that they'd blow up a fifty-cent test tube or something. He could end up fried. Or lost in another galaxy.

"Ready?" his teacher asked. "It's now or never!" Langston tried to slow down his heart rate just by thinking about it. But it was no use.

"Ready," he said, though it came out more like a croak than a word.

Mrs. Centauri aimed the giant laser at him and pushed a red button marked GREEN LASER ON.

"Woof! Woof! Howoooo!" Sirius 1 and Sirius 2 barked, then howled in unison, as if the laser made a piercing noise that only they could hear.

Langston saw a bright green flash of blurry light, almost like he was going past a forest of trees very fast in a car. He levitated straight up off the floor and catapulted out the dome right into the night sky as if he'd been hurled by a slingshot.

CHAPTER XII

Langston was hurtling through space at the speed of light.

The weird thing was that he could still see exactly what everything looked like—almost as if he were standing still. Langston couldn't figure out if this meant that Einstein's general theory of relativity was right or wrong. All he knew was that he was scared out of his gourd.

"Yeowwwww!" Langston screamed as he whizzed past a huge misshapen potato-looking rock he recognized as Mars's moon Phobos, missing it by only a few yards. *Phobos means* fear, Langston thought. *Somebody sure had* that *right!*

It's true, he thought, *it's really true. In space no one can hear you scream. What they don't tell you is that you can't even hear yourself scream! Yeowwwwww!*

Langston boomeranged around Phobos's gravity

field, past some American space junk left over from an old space mission, and slingshotted toward a big, holey rock in the asteroid belt. He was heading straight for it! Mrs. Centauri hadn't warned him about this.

Langston said a quick prayer and thought about how Mrs. Centauri would explain his disappearance to his parents. "Well, he went to get a granola bar from the vending machine in the basement of the planetarium, and he just never came back. . . ."

As the asteroid loomed in front of him, Langston scrunched his eyes shut and braced for the impact.

But to his surprise, it was a little like landing on a feather bed. He'd forgotten that he was just a hologram— a walking, talking beam of light. *And holograms don't feel pain,* Langston realized.

Actually, his soft landing was more like landing on a trampoline than a feather bed, because the collision bounced him right back out into space, twice as fast as before. And before long Langston figured out that this was just what Mrs. Centauri had been counting on. She'd told him she was going to bounce him off of one asteroid after another like a giant pinball. He'd be going faster and faster with each bounce, so he could travel to other galaxies in a matter of minutes instead of millennia. And he'd go deeper into space—where light beams that had left Earth more than a century ago could still be seen, giving him a spectacular window back in time.

Way out past the planet Pluto, Langston sailed by a real live UFO—a spaceship! It was about ten feet wide and shaped like a silver metal funnel.

During a brief slowdown in his trajectory Langston got a closer look at the spaceship. It had some sort of drawings on a metal plaque bolted to its side! One of them looked like a diagram of the hyperfine transition of an atom—maybe hydrogen. And what was that? A drawing of alien life-forms that didn't look so different from men and women on Earth! The alien man's hand was raised in greeting, as if he were saying, "Hello. Take me to your leader."

Wow! Langston thought. *Real space creatures! Wait till Mrs. Centauri hears about this!*

As he accelerated out of range, Langston felt sorry he hadn't thought to check out if the spaceship had any windows so he could get a look inside. Maybe there were some weird-looking aliens holed up in there. He sure wished he'd brought his camera along with him. But at least he was getting a good look at the side of the ship as he sailed away. It had words written on it!

"'Pioneer X?'" Langston read aloud, puzzled.

Oops. Now he really felt like a doofus. This was an American spaceship he'd read about that had been launched in 1972. It wasn't Pioneer *X*, it was Pioneer *Ten*! He could just imagine Mrs. Centauri laughing at him if he'd been dumb enough to tell her about his UFO discovery.

Langston's voyage finally came to a sudden halt, and he hung suspended in the dead silence of space. Langston realized he was probably 144.75 light-years away from home by now—at least, he was if Mrs. Centauri's plan had worked.

He tried to think about what to do next. His brain felt kind of slow, as if the faster he'd traveled, the dumber he'd gotten. He rolled upside down in the weightlessness of space for a moment so that he could get more blood to his brain. But it didn't do any good.

Langston finally remembered the telescope Mrs. Centauri had given him! Flipping right side up again, he put the scope to his eye and aimed it in the general direction of the Milky Way galaxy. About three quarters of the way across the 100,000-light-year-diameter galaxy, along the arm of the constellation Orion, Langston located a familiar but rather average star. From there he aimed the telescope to one of the planets orbiting it, a bluish point of light. The light came from a medium-size planet, the third one from that star, the Sun. Langston smiled. Home.

Earth looked so peaceful from way out here.

CHAPTER XIII

Langston stepped up the magnification on his telescope, aiming it toward the east coast of a continent in the Northern Hemisphere, and turned the focus ring.

And—kowabunga!—coming sharply into view were horses pulling buggies on cobblestone streets, people wearing strange, old-fashioned clothing, and a construction scaffolding for a big white building with a half-finished dome.

"The Capitol!" Langston said. "The way it looked when it wasn't all built yet!"

Now he could really be sure he was seeing Earth—Washington, D.C.—the way it looked back in the 1860s. It was nighttime, and the streets were lit with gas lamps.

Langston adjusted the aim of his telescope and stepped up the magnification another notch. He made out the individual red bricks of a building. He could even read the small type on a playbill posted outside it:

FORD'S THEATRE
OUR
AMERICAN
COUSIN
Starring Miss Laura Keene

Langston's view traveled through the window of the theater.

He focused more widely on the theater's stage, on which some actors were playing a scene. The audience appeared to be laughing. *So it must be a comedy,* Langston thought. *Let's hope so, anyway.*

Langston tilted his scope upward to the balcony and saw a theater box decorated with five flags, a portrait of George Washington hanging between two of them. *There must be important people sitting there,* Langston guessed, *to be in such fancy seats.* Inside the box was a pretty young lady with her hair tied back in a bun, sitting next to a handsome young man with a droopy mustache who held himself straight as a ramrod and had a military bearing even though he wasn't wearing a uniform. *He's probably a Civil War army officer,* Langston concluded.

Sitting next to the young couple was an older lady, very elegant in a flowing black dress. The old guy sitting next to her took her hand. She smiled at him, and her cheeks colored slightly in a blush. *That must be her husband.*

Langston raised his scope, turning the power up a notch to look at the old man's face. But the magnification was too high, and all he could see was a big nose and part of the man's rugged, stubbly-bearded chin, flocked with gray hairs. He had a mole on one cheek, and his lips were curled in a gentle smile. *Look at all those wrinkles on him!* Langston thought. *This guy sure looks like he's lived through hell!* Langston pulled back on the scope's magnification a little to get a better view of the man's whole face.

Holy moly! It was like looking at the face on a five-dollar bill come to life. *Abraham Lincoln!*

Suddenly the door at the back of the box opened. A good-looking young man with a mustache, wearing spurs and riding boots, strode through it. He raised his right hand, only inches from the back of the red rocking chair in which President Lincoln was sitting. The man had something in his hand, but Langston couldn't see what it was, since it was blocked by the president's head.

Oh, no! It's John Wilkes Booth!

"Booth—stop!" Langston screamed, even though he knew no one could hear him. "Look out, Mr. President! Noooooo!"

CHAPTER XIV

Langston had never felt so helpless in his whole life. *Well, maybe only once before,* he thought, remembering Neely.

A big puff of smoke rose from the theater box. Langston strained to see through it. President Lincoln's right arm flew up, then fell limply to his side. He slumped over, his wife, Mary, tenderly cradling his head, trying in vain to lift him upright. Her mouth was formed into a scream.

The young army officer wrestled with Booth, blocking a vicious knife stab to his chest. Booth slashed the officer's arm; the wounded man staggered backward onto a couch, then struggled to his feet. Booth leaped off the balcony. As he did, one of his spurs got caught in a blue flag draped over the box, and the army officer made a desperate grab for Booth's coattails. The assassin tore free, landing on the stage off-kilter. He shoved aside a startled actor, who took off running, then Booth stopped briefly to shout something at the audience. He limped as fast as he could off the stage.

The audience must have thought it was all part of the play. They didn't stop laughing until President Lincoln's companions up in the balcony started yelling and pointing at the stage. Now the audience stood, shouting and waving their arms. "Stop that man!" they seemed to be screaming. Some of them ran onto the stage, but it was too late. Booth was already gone.

Two distinguished-looking men burst through the door in the balcony box and rushed to President Lincoln's aid. They were probably doctors. But Langston knew from reading history books that the president couldn't be saved. He would be carried to the house across the street and laid in a bed much too small for a man so tall—and so important. And he would die the next morning.

CHAPTER XV

Suddenly Langston found himself actually standing back on Earth—in modern L.A. Or at least it looked like L.A.—the streets of South Central at night. And he had no idea how he had gotten there.

About a hundred feet ahead of him he saw the back of a kid who was walking just like Neely. Wait a minute! It *was* Neely! *But that's impossible,* Langston thought. *Must be my eyes playing tricks on me.*

Langston passed by a newspaper dispenser. He glanced at the headline: 12-YEAR-OLD GUNNED DOWN BY GANG MEMBERS. *Hey—that's the same . . .*

Langston knelt down in front of the machine for a closer look. The same photo of the Vipers kid. And the date: January 10, 2010. The day Neely had gotten shot!

It's last Sunday! Langston realized. *Somehow I've gone back a few days in time. That means Neely is still . . .*

"Wait!" Langston screamed, tearing down the street after the teenager. "Neely—stop!"

The young man kept walking for a while, then turned around.

"Lang! What you doin' out past your bedtime?"

It is *Neely. Thank you, Jesus!*

"Don't move!" Langston called with desperation. "Just stay right there!"

"Huh? You gone wacko, Jacko?"

Langston ran toward Neely—so hard and fast his lungs burned. As he got closer, he could see Neely was carrying a copy of the same newspaper in his hand.

"Neely!" Langston said between gasps of breath. "Don't . . . don't go down . . . down this street. I can see the future, man! You'll . . . you'll get shot. You'll die!"

"You really have gone wacko," Neely said, shaking his head. "Look, man—I gotta go meet . . . somebody." He turned around and started walking away. "See you in the loony bin, bud."

"No!" Langston chased after him and grabbed his arm. "It's the truth! Neely—trust me! You gotta believe me, man!"

Neely could see his friend was serious, even if he *had* gone crazy.

"Okay, okay, man," he said, putting a hand on Langston's shoulder. "Keep your shirt on. I won't go. Okay?"

Langston breathed a sigh of relief. He took a quick glance around to make sure they weren't being followed, and Langston led Neely away.

CHAPTER XVI

Langston felt something warm, sticky, and wet touching his face. He opened his eyes.

The first thing he saw was Sirius 1, who was licking his cheek.

"Yech!" Langston said, sitting upright and pushing the dog off him. "Get him off me!"

"He's awake, Mom!" Alpha called over her shoulder. She turned back to Langston. "You snore, you know."

Langston's head felt a little woozy, like the time he had taken some codeine medicine for bronchitis, but otherwise he was all right. He was sitting on a couch in Mrs. Centauri's house. That much was clear. But he wasn't sure of anything else.

Mrs. Centauri entered the room and knelt by the side of the couch.

"How're you feeling, kiddo?"

"Okay," he said. "I mean, like me."

"Good. Can you tell me what you remember?"

Langston lay back down and rubbed his temples.

"President Lincoln got shot. And I couldn't stop it!"

"You already told me," Mrs. Centauri said. "I'm so sorry you saw that, Lang. Please believe me, I picked that April date at random. I would never have sent you there if I'd known that—"

"You say I already told you?"

"Uh-huh. You were awake for a while when I put you in reverse and brought you back. Then you slept like a log. Guess you've got a touch of amnesia. That happens sometimes."

"I tried to save Neely!" Langston said, remembering. "And I did!"

Mrs. Centauri shook her head. "That part's not real, I'm afraid. Just a dream."

"No!" Langston said, sitting up again. "It's real! It's gotta be! He's alive!"

"Oh, Lang," Mrs. Centauri said, putting a hand on his shoulder. "Take it easy."

Langston leaped off the couch.

"No!" he said. "Look—I'll prove it!"

He ran toward a telephone on Mrs. Centauri's desk.

"Lang—don't!"

But it was too late. He had dialed a number.

"Mrs. Neubardt?" he said when somebody on the other end picked up. "Is . . . Neely there, please? I've got to talk to him!"

There was a long pause on the other end. Then a woman's loud voice: "Who . . . who is this? What kind of sick joke . . ." The woman slammed the phone down.

Langston walked back over to the couch and slowly slumped into it.

"I tried to warn you," Mrs. Centauri said sadly.

But Langston wasn't ready to give up yet.

"All right, if Neely was a dream, then how do you know I didn't dream the other stuff too? About traveling in space and time. Seeing Abe Lincoln! I read all that stuff in a book once. Maybe none of this really happened!"

"Well, for one thing . . . ," Mrs. Centauri said, plucking some small gray specks from Langston's jacket.

"What's that?"

"Space dust," she said, showing him the particles. "It's all over you."

"Maybe it's just regular old dust," Langston said defiantly.

"And for another thing . . ." Mrs. Centauri pointed across the room to a chair.

Langston's shell was sitting there, smiling dopily at him.

"Oh," Langston said, defeated.

Then he did something he hadn't done since the night Neely died. He cried.

CHAPTER XVII

"I should have stopped it from happening!" Langston moaned, embarrassed that Mrs. Centauri should see him like this. Everything, all the pain he'd been holding in for the past week, came tumbling out.

"It's not your fault," she said, handing him a handkerchief with a NASA logo embroidered on it. "You tried to get Neely to quit the gang. You did everything a friend could do."

"It *is* my fault!" Langston said, wiping his nose. "I got him so mad he confronted that bastard and got himself shot for it."

"You couldn't have known that would happen. Neely wouldn't want you beating up on yourself like this."

"I gotta do something!" Langston said. *"Something . . ."*

Sirius 1 waddled over and nuzzled Langston. He patted the dog absentmindedly.

. . . . .

Langston was suspended upside down by his ankles inside the barrel of Mrs. Centauri's giant telescope. Even at fourteen Langston was taller than his teacher—in fact, he was the tallest ninth grader at Banneker High—and she needed someone tall for this job.

"A little to the left . . . a little more . . . ," she guided him as he wiped part of the telescope's giant reflecting lens with a lint-free cloth. "Bingo! That spot's been driving me nuts. Like I've had a thing in my eye for the past month!"

Langston was nearly finished polishing the lens.

"Mrs. Centauri-tauri-tauri?" His voice echoed as he talked down the telescope tube.

"Hmm?"

Langston turned his head toward the open end of the tube to stop the echo.

"What if I don't want to just *watch* history from space? What if I wanted to . . ."

"Wanted to what?"

"What if I wanted to *make* history? I mean, like, change it around."

"Lang, the only way you're going to make history is when they give you the Nobel Prize. Remember what I said in class? One object can't occupy two different places at the same time. Basic physics. That goes for people, too. You can't be *watching* history and be *in* it at the same time."

"Huh?"

"Look at it this way . . . ," Mrs. Centauri said. "You can't see Earth's past unless you're looking at it from outer space a gazillion miles away, right? But if you're way out there in space, how can you also be on Earth at the same time, messing around with historical events?" Mrs. Centauri shrugged. "After all, there's only one of you."

"What about me and my shell?" Langston asked. "Isn't that me being in two places at once?"

Mrs. Centauri shook her head. "Nope. Your shell isn't really *you*. It's more like when a snake molts and leaves its old skin behind. Like I said, you can't be in two places at once. Simply put, my dear Watson, it's impossible."

"Impossible," Langston repeated. "Oh."

Mrs. Centauri pulled him by his ankles out of the telescope barrel. She looked at her watch. "It's really late. We'd better think about getting you home. Your folks must be getting worried about you."

"My mom sure will be, anyway. Don't worry. I'll explain it. Well, some of it."

She nodded, smiling. "We'll just fuse you back together with your shell, and then I'll phone a cab for you. My treat."

"Thanks. A cab . . . won't that be expensive?"

"Well, it would be, except that it's not really a cab. I've got a deal worked out with a guy who drives a milk truck. . . ."

CHAPTER XVIII

The next night Langston was on the sidewalk outside his parents' apartment, staring helplessly at a flat tire on his father's ramshackle old car. And though it was cold January out, he was sweating like it was July.

"I . . . can't," Langston said.

"Oh, really now," his father said, crossing his arms, "you can't. That so? And why might that be?"

Langston didn't know what to say. It seemed that almost anything he said would be wrong. His father moved closer, towering over him.

"Tire's here. Tire's flat. Flat as a pancake. You're here. Nice big strapping young man. What's the problem?"

"Don't . . . know how," Langston replied in a voice barely above a whisper.

"What's that, boy?"

"I said I don't know how."

"Oh. I see. You don't know how. He's fourteen years

old, and he don't know how to change a little bitty tire. I see."

Langston felt ashamed.

"Your mama out driving you one day, drives over a nail, and tire goes flat. And what will my boy say? 'Sorry, Mama. You get out and change it yourself. With your arther-itis and all. 'Cause I don't know how.' Is that it?"

Langston's teeth started to chatter.

"Couldn't be 'cause I got a son who spends more time lookin' at the moon than learnin' the stuff we mortal folk gotta learn to make do? Couldn't be 'cause he got his head in the clouds?"

Langston's shoulders slumped. His father handed him a tire iron.

"Nah. Couldn't be that. Go ahead. What are you waiting for?"

"I . . . said I can't!" Langston handed the tire iron back to his father. "I can't! I told you I was sorry I got home so late last night. Mrs. Centauri—"

"No back talk from you! Always talking back. No respect. And I don't want to hear no more about that Mrs. Centauri!"

"You . . . you don't understand!" Langston said. "You'll never understand! I got dreams. I don't want to be like . . ."

Langston knew he had made a terrible mistake. But it

was too late to take it back. His father stared daggers at him. He knew what Langston had meant, what he had been going to say.

Langston screwed up his courage and took things a step further. "You'll be fixing cars for the rest of your life!"

His father looked stung for a moment, then recovered his bearings. He spoke to Langston in a quiet tone—scarier, somehow, than if he'd shouted back.

"Maybe I will. Maybe I will. I'm just a poor, uneducated mechanic who fixes fancy cars for rich white folk. Yeah. But I put food in the mouth of you and your mama. And don't you ever—don't you *ever*—forget it, boy."

They moved toward each other in a flash, coiled up like snakes ready to strike. Would he hit his father first, or would his father hit him? His father was bigger. He had a tire iron. Would he use it on his own son?

"What's going on here!"

Langston's mother, hair arranged for bed, stepped out on the street in her bathrobe and moved quickly between her husband and her son. She had some kind of mother wit, an uncanny instinct for knowing when trouble was brewing.

"Put that thing down!" she demanded, pointing toward the tire iron.

"What you say? You know I'd never hit the boy!"

"Put it down, Horace!"

Langston's mother stood there between her two tall

men like a great wall of sheer willpower, defying them to lay a hand on each other.

Finally both father and son took a step backward, lowering their hands. But their eyes stayed locked together in a powerful kind of rage as old as the universe.

A few minutes later, Langston was sitting in the living room, angrily flipping the pages of *Asimov's Science Fiction* magazine. He heard the front door slam. It was a familiar sound. It made the dishes rattle.

"Why does he have to slam doors like that?" he said.

"Your father comes from a long line of door slammers, honey," his mother replied, "but he's a good man."

Langston gave her a skeptical look.

"Now, I know that look," she said. "You'll know he is a good man someday. He's just trying to protect you. Doesn't want to see you get hurt—"

"Yeah, sure."

"Hurt by life. I married a young man once," his mother said, smiling at the memory. "He had dreams, oh yes, he had dreams. Dreams as big as a church picnic in Bible country."

"You were married to someone before Dad?"

She laughed quietly, shaking her head. "You know, you and he are like two peas in a pod. If I were a gambling woman, I'd bet that's why you're at each other so much."

Langston just shrugged.

"He's been wanting to tell you how he feels, you know," she said. "About you losing your friend. It's just that . . . his head don't always know his heart's way of speaking."

"It's not that hard."

"For him it is. He wasn't raised up to know."

Langston found this hard to accept. He changed the subject. "Ma, let's say there's something you want to do. Bad. And somebody—somebody smart you got a lot of respect for—tells you you can't. That it's impossible."

Langston's mother tilted her head back and seemed to be reaching for something way back in her memory.

"Bring me all of your dreams,
 You dreamers,
 Bring me all of your
 Heart melodies
 That I may wrap them
 In a blue cloud-cloth
 Away from the too-rough fingers
 Of the world."

Langston's mother sighed.

"You write that?" he asked her.

She shook her head. "It was written by your name-sake, honey. Langston Hughes."

CHAPTER XIX

Moonlight streamed through Langston's bedroom window. He was sitting on his bed, looking at the only photo he had of himself and Neely. They were smiling, standing side by side, legs tied together with rope, arms around each other's shoulders. It had been taken about a year ago, when they had won a three-legged race together at school—a great moment, when they'd worked as a team. Though he had to admit, it was more like a two-legged race, since Neely was faster and was almost dragging Langston along. But they'd won. And if Langston had had a brother of his own, it would have felt something like it did that day with him and Neely.

Langston sighed and put the photo on the night-stand. He took out and cleaned his contact lenses and lay down in bed.

Shortly after he fell asleep, someone opened his door. Langston's father entered the room and stood over him, watching the slow rise and fall of his son's chest. And had Langston been awake at the time, he would have seen the love in his father's eyes.

Langston's father put something in the pocket of the boy's Anaheim Angels jacket, which was draped over a chair. Then he left, shutting the door quietly behind him.

The next morning, Langston awoke with a start. A bright beam of sunlight was glaring right in his eyes, and when he sat up in bed, he saw his reflection in the two mirrors in his room—one by the door, the other above his desk. Two side-by-side identical images of himself. He looked back and forth between one copy of himself and the other.

Mrs. Centauri's words echoed in his head: "If you're way out there in space, how can you also be on Earth at the same time, messing around with historical events? After all, there's only one of you. . . . Like I said, you can't be in two places at once. Simply put, my dear Watson, it's impossible."

Langston just kept staring at his reflections in the mirrors.

"One object, in two different places . . . ," he whispered.

Suddenly a light seemed to turn on inside Langston's brain.

He got dressed hurriedly and tore through the living room carrying one of the big mirrors from his bedroom, heading for the door.

His mother grabbed him on the fly.

"Whoa, young man! What you doing with that thing? Where you going at this hour on a Saturday morning with two different color socks on?"

Langston looked down at his feet. She was right that his socks didn't match, but there was no time to change them. He gave her a quick kiss on the cheek.

"Don't worry, Mama. I'll be all right."

He dashed out the door before she could say anything else. Langston's mother just stood there shaking her head.

"Thanks for the lift, man," Langston said as the hippie milkman helped unload the mirror from the back of the truck at Mrs. Centauri's house.

"Peace, brother," the milkman replied, holding up two fingers in a V. "Catch you later, gator, when I deliver the moo juice. My cows were havin' a sit-down strike this morning. Must want more overtime!" He glanced down at Langston's feet and smiled. "Dig your socks, man."

He drove away.

Langston approached the house. There was a note on the door for the milkman. He hoped that might mean nobody was home. Discovering the door was unlocked again, he turned the knob and stepped inside.

"Mrs. Centauri? Alpha?"

After leaning the mirror against a wall, Langston

moved cautiously through the room, peeking around corners, checking behind doors.

Good. Nobody here. That was just what Langston had been counting on.

Sirius 2 greeted him, growled, but didn't cause any trouble. Sirius 1 was snoozing on the couch.

Langston decided that before taking his plan any farther, he ought to crunch some numbers. He sat down at the computer console that operated the giant laser in the observatory. Apparently Mrs. Centauri had retracted the telescope into the basement before going out. And she'd left the dome open!

Langston used the keyboard to type in the date— January 16, 2010.

"Distance in light-years to destination?"

Light-years? Langston thought. *I only want to go back a week! To the day Neely died.*

"Let's see . . . ," he said aloud. "One day is one three-hundred-sixty-fifth of a light-year. So seven days is seven times that. . . ."

He whipped his pocket calculator out from his shirt pocket beneath his sweater, entered some numbers, and multiplied. Then he typed the result on the computer keyboard.

".019178 light-years."

The computer made a *boing!* noise.

"Invalid entry! Minimum possible distance of destination in light-years: 100."

"A hundred years!" Langston said. "Damn!"

This was something he sure hadn't planned on. He slammed his fist on the console. "Now I'll never be able to save Neely. . . ."

Back in the living room Langston noticed Alpha's toy gun sitting on the desk right where her mother had left it. He picked it up and turned it over slowly in his hand. Yes, it was only a child's plastic toy, but the real ones had brought the world nothing but misery. He hated its ugly, snub-nosed shape. He hated everything about it. Most of all, he wished the damn thing had never been invented!

"Wait a minute . . . ," Langston said, an idea forming in his brain. "That's it!"

Langston dashed over to Mrs. Centauri's PC.

He closed the screen's open window—which showed an article about dinosaurs—then skimmed the folder titles on the computer's desktop: School Papers, Mom's Recipes, Solar Eclipse Forecasts, NASA Newsletters . . . . Langston didn't see anything helpful, but he kept looking.

Ah—here's something! he thought at last. *Just what I need.* He double-clicked on another folder.

A full-color window popped open, along with some words on the screen. *"Welcome to the Junior Electronic Encyclopedia of Science and Technology. Please type in the letter of the volume you would like to see."*

Langston typed in the letter *G.*

"Thank you. Have fun!" a deep computer voice said.

Oh, God, Langston thought. *Just what I need. A corny talking computer.*

Langston scanned down the list of *G* entries: *Galaxy, Gestation, Goldfish.* . . . He clicked on a word farther down the list.

"Guns: see Firearms."

Langston sighed and clicked on *Firearms.*

KABOOM!

The startling sound of a cannon going off came from the computer's speakers, and Langston practically leaped from his chair. Images of guns, from the most primitive to the most advanced, flashed on the monitor.

Langston read the beginning of the encyclopedia article: *"History records that guns were invented in what is now Morocco around the year 1300. . . ."*

Langston's jaw set in rigid determination.

"Not if I can help it," he muttered.

Langston set up the mirror directly opposite Mrs. Centauri's iridium laser. He took a deep breath, then pressed the start button and ran as fast as he could to the center of the circle in which he'd stood two days before. He made sure to stand right on the *X*.

A moment later Langston looked behind him and stood face-to-face with a holographic image. It was an exact copy of him—made of light, just as he now was—

except it was was reversed, like a mirror image. And it moved in perfect sync with him.

The mirror had worked! He'd actually divided himself into two identical holograms!

Langston moved his hand to scratch an itch, and his mirror-image hologram did the same thing. And over on the couch was the *other* copy of Langston—his useless shell—sleeping peacefully with his arm around Sirius 1.

So far, so good. But Langston knew the hard part of the experiment was really only just beginning. And suddenly he wasn't sure any of this was such a good idea. After all, he hadn't worked out the details. Something might go kablooey.

Langston took a deep breath and went over his plan again.

Step one: bounce myself and my holographic "twin" out into space, seven hundred and ten light-years away. Light waves that left Earth back when guns were invented are just now arriving there, carrying images of Earth in medieval times. Then, while my twin is looking through the little telescope at Earth as it was in the year 1300, I'll bounce myself right back into the past events he's looking at. It'll be like watching history from a gazillion miles away—and being in it at the same time. It's a no-brainer!

Langston glanced over at his lazy shell, who was snoring on the couch, and then at his reversed hologram, who was staring alertly right back at him.

But what if everything gets screwed up? Langston worried. *What if when this is all over, I can't glue the three of us back together again? What if when my two holograms go out into space, it's like a one-way ticket to nowhere? I'll never see my mother again—or Mrs. Centauri. Or see the Anaheim Angels play baseball. Me and my holographic twin might end up stuck in some freaky galaxy forever, drifting along like old space junk!*

But there was no time to worry so much about any of this creepy stuff now.

He had only one chance to save Neely, and he had to take it!

With his holographic twin trotting after him, Langston went back into Mrs. Centauri's observatory and opened a beautiful old atlas.

He turned to a map of Africa. Two fingers, one from each Langston hologram, traced the latitude and longitude of Morocco.

The two Langstons approached the console of the giant laser.

"Distance in light-years to destination?" the computer asked.

They typed in, *"710."* The keyboard was pretty crowded with four hands typing on it at once.

"Hey! Watch where you put those fingers!" the original Langston complained.

"Coordinates?"

They entered the latitude and longitude of their destination and waited for the results.

"Earth view: Fez, Morocco, January 16, 1300."

The original Langston hunted around the room until he finally found a device that looked like a small TV clicker and was labeled LASER REMOTE CONTROL.

The two Langstons stood in front of the giant green laser in Mrs. Centauri's observatory. Standing on their mark, they competed to be the first to press the button on the laser remote control.

It was a tie.

In another second the Langstons were shot like two cannonballs into the deep, silent blackness of space, ricocheting off of asteroids.

"Yeowwwwwwwwwww!" they screamed in unison.

Meanwhile, back in Mrs. Centauri's house, hundreds of light-years away, the *Electronic Encyclopedia* flashed a message on the computer's bright blue screen: *"Thank you. Have a nice day!"*

CHAPTER XX

The two Langstons lurched to a stop in the middle of a beautiful yellow spiral nebula that shone brightly against the inky background of space. The nebula was so interesting that the original Langston felt like hanging around awhile to study it, but he realized there was no time to waste. He put the laser remote control device in his Anaheim Angels jacket pocket so he'd have it later to get back to Earth.

Fortunately the original Langston had remembered to bring along Mrs. Centauri's powerful little telescope. He wasn't sure he could trust the other Langston to think about practical things like that.

He handed the telescope to the other Langston and asked him to take a look at Earth. The original Langston had to go through the motions of using the optical instrument so that his mirror image would copy him.

"After you," the other Langston said, handing back the telescope.

"No. After *you*," the original Langston said, handing it back again.

Well, they certainly were learning how to get along better. But they kept apologizing and passing the telescope back and forth, over and over again, until finally the original Langston had to put a stop to it.

"Enough!"

"Enough!" the other Langston repeated, shrugging and aiming the telescope toward North Africa, focusing the lens.

Sure enough, he reported, he could see lots of sand, guys in long robes—and no cars or fast-food restaurants anyplace. Langston had no idea what the year 1300 should look like and he'd never been to Morocco, but as far as he could tell, this seemed like the place. He took turns with his twin, looking through the scope at Morocco.

They saw two large, chaotic groups of men rushing furiously toward each other, then every few seconds a man would stop suddenly in his tracks, grimace in pain, and fall to the ground. It looked like the Moroccans were fighting some kind of war. *Well, some things never change,* Langston thought.

Langston removed the laser remote control from his pocket and examined the buttons on it. Just to be on the safe side, he punched in the date—January 16, 1300—and the coordinates of Morocco. Then he looked at the other choices.

One button was labeled DOUBLE VOYAGER EARTH RETURN. That didn't sound very promising. He didn't want to send *both* Langstons back to Earth—at least not right now.

Another button said SOLO VOYAGER EARTH RETURN. *Bingo!* That sounded like a likely candidate.

Langston held his breath and pressed the solo button.

A second later the original Langston found himself catapulted back out into space, leaving the other Langston—who was still looking at Morocco's past through the telescope—far behind.

As they moved farther and farther apart in the vast reaches of space, the two Langstons waved good-bye to each other. Or at least it looked that way. Maybe the other Langston was really just copying what his twin was doing.

The original Langston felt kind of sad at this temporary parting. It had really almost been like having a brother for a little while.

CHAPTER XXI

Langston heard a whizzing noise near his right ear and ducked. A flaming arrow shot past, missing him by just a few inches!

He had landed back on Earth in what looked like a giant sandbox. Everywhere there were Middle Eastern–looking men in long robes firing arrows at one another and shouting things in a language Langston couldn't understand.

Everybody seemed too busy fighting to notice the strange way Langston had arrived—or even that he was there at all.

A man who seemed to be some sort of general—he was giving everybody else orders—called one of the soldiers over. He motioned toward three burlap sacks that were filled with powders of different colors—yellow, black, and white—and told the soldier to do something with them.

Langston stood up, brushed himself off, and glanced around. He wanted to see what kinds of weapons the men were using.

He saw only arrows and swords. That was good news. But everywhere there was the sound of wounded men screaming in pain. And the sharp smell of dead soldiers' bodies baking in the hot African sun made Langston sick to his stomach.

An officer, apparently nearsighted and mistaking Langston for a soldier, rushed over and shoved a heavy sack in Langston's arms, knocking him over. Then the man gave him some sort of order in Arabic, motioning toward the other sacks.

Langston had no idea what the guy wanted from him, but he could see there were now several soldiers pouring and mixing the powders together into a giant barrel. He walked over to join them, dragging the sack and hoping that if he seemed to be doing something useful, he wouldn't attract any special attention.

Langston heard a rumbling sound and turned just in time to see an oxcart rolling toward him on big wooden wheels. On the cart was a large, hollow tube made of black metal and tilted up at a forty-five-degree angle. There were some round things next to it that looked like small bowling balls.

"It's a cannon!" Langston exclaimed. "Oh, no! I'm too late!"

Several men stared at him strangely.

Before Langston could think about what to do next, one of the other soldiers, who had a droopy-jowled face that reminded Langston of a camel, grabbed him roughly by the arm and forced a shovel into his hand. The soldier was yelling at him like he wanted Langston to get back to work.

Langston shoveled and mixed the powders together. After all, these didn't look like guys he wanted mad at him.

On an impulse Langston licked his fingertip, then lightly brushed it against the mixed powder, picking up a few grains. He sniffed at his finger, then quickly touched it to his tongue.

He immediately recognized the smell and acrid taste. It was the same thing Mrs. Centauri had mixed one day when she was subbing for Mr. Weishaus in chemistry class.

"Gunpowder!"

Langston hadn't gone back nearly far enough in time! He was too late to prevent the invention of guns, but even worse, he now understood that stopping the invention of guns wouldn't be enough. As long as there was gunpowder, guns could always be invented. And he had no idea how long gunpowder had been around.

Langston was jolted from his thoughts when the work supervisor gave him another sharp yank on the arm.

"Yo! Camel Face!" Langston snapped, in no mood to be trifled with. "Cut that out!"

The soldier stared at him, a very puzzled look on his droopy face. And in the next second he looked even more surprised. For that was when Langston pressed the Double Voyager Earth Return button on the laser remote control and rocketed himself back into space.

CHAPTER XXII

Langston sat at Mrs. Centauri's computer. The other Langston—which had returned safely to 2010 with him—and their shell sat on the couch across the room playing Go Fish. Of course, the shell was losing.

It was a card game for idiots. *Well,* Langston thought as he watched them, *at least I've finally cured Mirror Man of copying everything I do.*

Langston looked at an *Electronic Encyclopedia* article on the computer screen.

"Gunpowder was invented by the Chinese sometime before the eleventh century, but it was not usable in firearms until Englishman Roger Bacon, a Franciscan friar and scientist who lived in the 1200s, discovered the formula for gunpowder, made a few changes to it, and wrote it down in code in a book."

So, this Bacon dude was the one! Langston switched to the *B* volume in the encyclopedia.

"Thank you! Have fun!" the computer voice said.

A new window popped open with an article about Roger Bacon. There was even a picture of the old guy. He was wearing a brown friar's habit and had a long, angular nose, close-cropped gray hair, and, Langston noted, a sharp look in his eye like he didn't take any crap from anybody. Langston realized this was one of the guys whose portraits hung on Mrs. Centauri's living-room wall.

Langston clicked a button so that the article would be read aloud to him.

"Meet the remarkable Roger Bacon," the deep computer voice said, "one of the world's first scientists, who was hundreds of years ahead of his time. Yes, many of the wonders of our own day—the submarine, the airplane, the automobile, gunpowder, and the telescope, for example—were predicted or invented by this wizard of the thirteenth century. . . ."

A swirl of images of these inventions fluttered across the computer screen.

"I thought da Vinci was the first one to think up the airplane . . . ," Langston muttered.

"Ah! You probably thought Leonardo da Vinci thought up the airplane, didn't you?"

"Smarty-pants," Langston grumbled.

"A Franciscan friar and professor at Oxford University, the outspoken Bacon (also known as

Doctor Mirabilis, which in Latin means 'wonderful teacher') was a strict believer in the scientific method and was frequently persecuted by his critics in the Church, who . . ."

Langston had heard enough. He made a printout of the article on Bacon, folded it, and slipped it into his Anaheim Angels jacket pocket.

Langston knew what he had to do.

"Come on, you," he said to the other Langston while his shell looked on dumbly. "We've got work to do."

CHAPTER XXIII

Oxford, England—January 16, 1278

An old man wearing a brown friar's habit, using a wooden crutch with one arm and carrying a box of glass prisms with the other, hobbled rapidly down the hallowed halls of Oxford University. As always, he was late for class.

His temperament was so unpleasant that he even seemed to breathe the air with a built-in sense of disapproval.

As he turned the corner of the hall, a tubby, near-sighted visiting professor crashed right into him.

The friar's crutch went flying out from under him, and he and his prisms tumbled to the sawdust-covered floor.

"Oh, pardon me, Brother!" the visiting professor said, mortified, trying to help the old man up. "And you, already injured!"

The old man got to his feet, struggling to free himself from the professor's meaty grasp.

"Unhand me, you beslubbering, beef-witted barnacle! And it's *Father,* not Brother! Any fool knows some friars are priests!"

"I beg your indulgence!" the professor sputtered, letting go of his arm. "Are you all right, Father . . . uh . . . Father . . ."

"Bacon. Roger Bacon," the man said, brushing the sawdust from his clothes and picking up the prisms that weren't broken. "I was in fine fettle till a few moments ago!"

"Not *Professor* Bacon? The Honorable Doctor Mirabilis?"

"The very same. Please try to contain your enthusiasm."

"Doctor Mirabilis, this *is* an honor!" The professor reached to shake hands. "Your reputation precedes you!"

Bacon was already hobbling away on the crutch, but the tubby professor chased after him.

"And it follows me," Bacon said sourly. "Relentlessly."

But the professor wouldn't take the hint.

"I've read about your experiments in optics. Is it true that you've been able to obtain a close view of celestial bodies using a glass—"

Bacon removed a watch from the pocket of his habit

and glanced at it. "My garrulous friend. You've consumed one minute and ten seconds of my time, during which I could have invented a horseless carriage. Good day."

And without further ado Dr. Bacon hobbled away.

The lecture hall was filled with students as young as fourteen and as old as twenty-five. They were all boys, of course, since girls in those days weren't allowed to go to Oxford.

As Dr. Bacon limped to the front of the class, the students buzzed about his injury.

"He probably tripped over his pride," a tall boy whispered to his classmate. They laughed.

The other Oxford professors began their lectures with a cheerful "Good morrow, young gentlemen" or a friendly "Good day." But Dr. Roger Bacon always jumped right in without any niceties.

"Experiment and observation," he began that morning. "That is the foundation of my scientific method."

Another friar stood with his arms crossed at the back of the room, coldly observing Dr. Bacon. If Bacon saw him there, he chose to ignore him.

"Never believe anything that you can't see with your own eyes," he continued.

"Doctor, does that include God?" a bushy-haired student interjected, challenging the professor with a smirk.

The friar at the back of the room leaned forward, watching Bacon intently.

The atmosphere grew tense as Bacon considered how to answer. He pointed out the window.

"I see God in every leaf on that tree," he replied. "I find it more difficult, I confess, to see God's handiwork in the person of students who ask impertinent questions."

The students laughed. The friar in the back of the room looked disappointed.

"What about the teachings of the Church?" a student in the front row asked. "Are we to believe only those things that can be proved by experiment and observation?"

Dr. Bacon knew he must watch his step. He caught the other friar's eye.

"No," he answered. "However, I have *observed* that whenever I *experiment* with heresy, I find myself in a good deal of trouble."

The students laughed again, but the friar at the back of the room didn't seem to see any humor in it.

Bacon hobbled back and forth on his crutch as he lectured.

"What the eyes can see, the mind can believe. But sometimes the eyes can deceive. . . ."

Bacon leaned his crutch against the wall. Then he walked—without any difficulty whatsoever—back to the front of the class.

The students gasped.

"As you can see, my 'injury' was a figment of your imagination. You saw, yes. But did you test and *observe*? No!"

The students gave him spontaneous applause for fooling them.

"The earth may appear flat, but I will someday be proved correct that it is round," Bacon said, "and it is *not* the center of the cosmos."

"That's heresy!" the friar shouted from the back, waving his fist.

All the students turned around. Bacon wasn't intimidated and spoke to the friar directly.

"Welcome to my classroom, Brother. Scholars, this is the general of my Franciscan order, Brother Jerome— Jerome of Ascoli. He has seen fit to grace us with his presence today."

Jerome glowered at Bacon. He knew he was being mocked, though he couldn't prove it. He left the room in a huff.

Bacon turned to the bushy-haired student. "What color is light?"

"White, of course!"

Bacon handed out the prisms among the students.

"Hold them up to the light," he instructed.

With sunlight streaming through them, the prisms cast rainbows all over the walls.

"Oooh!"

"Ahhh!"

The students murmured in wonderment. None of them had ever seen a prism before.

"Where is the rainbow?" Bacon asked. "In the glass or in the light? Or perhaps in your eye? Do your eyes deceive? Proceed to my laboratory."

Dr. Bacon and his students opened the door to his university lab. They stood staring in amazement for a moment, then Bacon slumped down onto a stool. The lab had been ransacked. Broken glass beakers and tubes littered the shelves. Red chemical liquids covered the floor like blood. All the tables had been overturned. The work of a dozen years was ruined.

"Doctor," a student cried, "who would do such a thing?"

Bacon didn't hesitate to reply. "My friends in the Church."

CHAPTER XXIV

In Oxford town a peasant woman carrying a basket of laundry passed by a pile of hay. There would have been nothing unusual about this, except for the fact that the hay was moving. All by itself. Curious, she stopped to stare at it.

Suddenly the hay pile erupted like a strange sort of volcano. A head emerged from the hay like Saint John the Baptist's on a platter, and the washerwoman ran screaming down the street.

The head belonged to Langston, as this was where fate—with a little help from Mrs. Centauri's laser machine—had dropped him. Langston stood up, brushed the hay off, and glanced around.

The first thing he noticed was a rotten smell. But what did he expect from a century that had horses instead of cars, no refrigerators to keep food from spoiling, and lots of people who hardly ever bathed and had never heard of deodorant?

The next thing he noticed was that everyone was noticing him. People were staring, their heads swiveling around as they passed by. They pointed rudely at him as if he were a two-headed turtle, and whispered among themselves.

At first Langston thought this unwelcome attention was on account of the way he was dressed. People here seemed to be wearing sacks that looked like they had once been used to store potatoes, and Langston certainly wasn't dressed like that. After a while, though, he realized that everyone here was white, and that was probably why they found him such a curiosity. It occurred to him that there were probably very few black people in Britain in the thirteenth century.

Pretty weird, he thought, that people who trained bears to dance and led them around on leashes like dogs, left piles of garbage to rot in the street, and believed that the best way to cure disease was to drive the devil out didn't think any of this odd—but found *him* strange.

Langston took the article about Dr. Roger Bacon from his pocket: "A Franciscan friar and professor at Oxford University, the outspoken Bacon (also known as Doctor Mirabilis, which in Latin means 'wonderful teacher') . . ."

Langston glanced around to see if there was anybody he could to talk to. Everyone seemed to be in such a big hurry, carrying baskets of food or loads of firewood, rushing here and there, or shooing pigs.

"A ha'penny? A ha'penny, kind master, for an old man's supper?"

A pitiable man in rags with bare, bleeding feet held out a grimy palm to Langston, a pleading look in his one remaining eye.

Poor guy, Langston thought. He reached into his pocket and handed him a coin.

"Blimey, what the dickens 'ave we got 'ere?" the old man said, tilting his head and staring at the face of George Washington on the quarter. "That ain't good old King Longshanks!" He bit the coin to see if it was real silver.

The old man put his nose in Langston's face and grabbed him forcefully by the wrist. "You wouldn't be tryin' to put one over on me, now would ya, master?"

"Uh . . . no, sir," Langston said nervously. "I'm afraid I haven't got anything else to give you. Sorry."

The old man threw the coin on the ground, spit on it, and shuffled away.

Just then a big wooden horse-drawn milk wagon crossed the street, splashing Langston with mud.

"Hey!" Langston leaped out of the way and landed on his knees in the mud.

The driver pulled up hard on the horses' reins.

"Meshuggener!" he shouted at Langston. "Have you no eyes to see where you walk?"

"Me?" Langston said, wondering what the man had

called him. "You're a lousy driver! I should have you arrested!"

"So. Now the *meshuggener* is some kind of *yatebedam*—a bigshot, eh?"

Langston got up and looked at the driver. He wore a long black coat and black hat and had a gray, bushy beard. He had his hands on his hips and was scowling.

Suddenly the old man's angry expression changed. He stared at Langston with a broad, toothy grin.

"The lost black tribe of Israel!" the man exulted.

Langston supposed the old man had never seen a black person before. He remembered reading somewhere that there had been a tribe of black Jews in Ethiopia, dating all the way back to biblical times. Come to think of it, the driver looked like the highly religious Orthodox Jews he'd seen sometimes in L.A.

The old man cleared some bundles off the seat next to him.

"Come, *mayn kind*!" he said, patting the seat. "You look all *oysgematert*. Take a rest! It will be a *mitsve* for me to take you wherever you're going."

Langston figured that it was probably safe to hitch a ride with this guy. Besides, he might be able to ask him some questions. He climbed up into the wagon, and they rode off.

The wagon bumped and swerved dangerously, barely missing the people and pigs in the street.

Langston hung on to the seat, but the old man seemed unperturbed.

"The One Above has sent us a beautiful day," he said. "Not a cloud in the sky."

"Uh . . . you wouldn't happen to be going to Oxford University, would you?" Langston asked.

The man didn't answer, but suddenly pressed his hand to his lower back.

"*Oy!* This milk I *shlep* every morning, here and there and here and there. It keeps *mein kinderlekh* clothed and fed. But *veh iz mir*—what it does to my spine!"

"I'm sorry to hear that," Langston said, not knowing what else to say.

"Pissht! No need to be sorry," he said. "My children give me *nakhes*, even for all the *tsores* they cause."

"Do any of them go to Oxford University?"

"Oxford! A Jew at Oxford?" the old man exclaimed, then muttered, "*Er bolbet narishkaytn!*"

"Huh?"

"I said, 'He talks nonsense.'"

"Oh," Langston replied, shrugging. "You see, I'd like to go to Oxford and—"

"*Mazel tov!* Good luck!"

"You wouldn't know how to get to Oxford University, would you?"

The old man leaned toward Langston. "Study, young man. Study!"

CHAPTER XXV

Within a quarter hour the wagon stopped in front of a big stone building.

"Wow!" Langston exclaimed. "It looks just like a castle!"

"We should all have such a house," the old man replied.

Langston hopped out of the wagon. The man shook his hand.

"You need help, you come find Old Man Rosenbloom, eh? In the house at Queen Street and Cornmarket—near the big clock tower in the center of town."

"Thanks! I'll be sure to come see you if I run into trouble."

"*Me?* I'm not Rosenbloom!" the man said, shrugging.

Langston looked puzzled.

"Just a little humor," the old man said with a smile. He gave a little flick to the horses' reins and rode away.

· · · · ·

Meanwhile, outside Mrs. Centauri's house the milkman was reading a note tacked to her door:

JERRY:
PLEASE LEAVE TWO QUARTS MILK AND
ONE CREAM. MUCHO THANKS.
    -MRS. CENTAURI

He followed her instructions, and just as he was closing the metal milk box the front door suddenly opened, nearly hitting him in the face, and somebody walked out.

"Well, if it isn't my bud, the Langster! How you doin', man?" the milkman said, slapping the boy on the back.

There was no response. "Say, would you tell Mrs. C. that she owes me for the past two weeks?"

The boy just stared at him blankly.

"You okay, man? You look like you're trippin'!"

The boy that looked like Langston walked right past the milkman as if he weren't there. He headed down the hill with a stiff, zombie-like gait.

"Need a lift?" the milkman called after him.

But the boy just ignored him and kept on walking.

The milkman shrugged.

Langston's mother was at home watching a talk show on television.

"There are aliens living among us, and they're called teenagers!" the man on the TV was saying.

"You got that right, Dr. Phil," Langston's mother muttered.

"Do you really know your kids? Do they know you? On today's show . . ."

There was a knock on the door. Langston's mother was so focused on her show that she didn't notice till the second knock. She eased herself off the couch and opened the door.

"Why didn't you use your key?" she said to the boy who looked like Langston.

There was no reply.

Langston's mother gave him a kiss on the forehead between his two glazed-over eyes and sat back down to watch TV. Langston's shell walked into the room with his robotic gait and sat down next to her on the couch.

"There's some leftover chicken in the fridge," she said without taking her eyes off the TV screen. "How was your day?"

The shell didn't say anything.

"That good, huh?"

"Teenagers are known to explore new things," Dr. Phil was saying, "but they don't make severe switches in personality just out of the blue. If they're making drastic behavioral changes, there's a reason."

The shell was flipping through *Asimov's Science Fiction* magazine, which he was holding upside down. Then he turned his head upside down so the magazine would be right side up. Langston's mother didn't notice.

"As a parent it's your responsibility to identify what's behind the change. It may be a recent event, or it may be something deep rooted. . . ."

"Hon," Langston's mother said, "take out the kitchen trash, please."

The boy who looked like Langston got up immediately and trotted toward the kitchen.

"Hmmph . . . ," she said with surprise, watching him go. "Must be doing something right."

Twenty minutes later, Langston's shell was standing on the roof of the housing project, throwing a toaster oven and half a dozen china plates onto a giant heap he'd created there. This was his fifth trip up from the kitchen. He kept trooping through the living room carrying out stacks of food and kitchen appliances. Like a robot on speed, he was throwing out the family's best china, silverware, cans of beans and boxes of oatmeal, the coffeemaker—anything he could find.

"You go, boy!" Langston's mother said to the TV screen, her attention fixed only on Dr. Phil.

CHAPTER XXVI

Langston strode confidently down the Great Hall at Oxford University. He hoped that if he looked like he belonged there, maybe people would think that he did. The guys he passed in the hallway were a mix of teachers and students.

Langston stopped a kindly-looking friar who was munching on what looked like the leg of a wild boar.

"Sir, could you tell me where I can find Dr. Roger Bacon?"

"He's taking confession," the man said, wiping his mouth on his sleeve, "in the chapel, three doors down to the left."

The professor scrutinized Langston.

"I don't recall having seen you here before, young man. What is your name?"

Langston gulped, hoping his brain wouldn't fail him.

"Uh . . . I'm one of the foreign exchange students.

From Ethiopia. Nice to meet you, Brother. I'd better get going."

Langston hurried down the hall before the friar could ask him any more questions.

A few minutes later Langston stood at the end of a long line of teenage boys who were waiting to give their confession. He couldn't see who was inside the confessional, since the doors to the wooden box were closed.

When no one was looking, Langston sneaked around to the back of the confessional and put his ear to the wall. He felt like a rat, snooping like this, but he needed to know if he'd come to the right place.

"Father, I . . . I have had impure thoughts," he heard a nervous boy saying, "about one of the girls who works in the kitchen."

"Have you acted on them?" a much deeper voice replied.

"No. Uh . . . well, yes, Father. She's with child. She says the baby is mine."

"Is she comely?"

"Yes, very, Father."

"I see. . . ."

Langston wondered how the priest would reply.

"Well, that's very understandable for a boy your age."

"Then . . . you . . . you've absolved me of my sin?" the boy asked eagerly.

"Yes, my son."

Well, Langston thought, *this guy certainly grades on a curve!*

"Thank you, Father!" the boy said, obviously relieved. He started to open the confessional door. Langston jumped back into the shadows. But then the boy seemed to change his mind when the priest spoke again.

"Anything else?" the priest asked.

"Nothing, Father. I should be going now. I did not do my science assignment, which was due yesterday, and—"

"WHAT!" the priest's voice thundered.

There was a *bang!* as the man stood up, apparently hitting his head on the ceiling of the confessional. "Bloody hell! Say one hundred Hail Marys and come back tomorrow!"

"Y-y-y-yes, Father."

"And your work damn well better be completed by then!"

This guy sure has an interesting set of priorities in the sin department, Langston thought. *And he certainly doesn't talk like a priest!*

Langston ducked around to the rear of the chapel and got back in line. The other kids moved up quickly in the queue—Langston heard an occasional outburst from the priest—and before long it was Langston's turn.

Nervous, he stepped inside the box, shut the door behind him, and sat down on the hard wooden seat.

"Dr. Bacon? I mean, Father?"

"Let's get to it, shall we? *Tempus fugit.*"

So it really was Dr. Bacon!

"Uh . . . I need to talk to you," Langston said.

"That is the general idea."

"No," Langston said. "I mean *really* talk to you."

"Do you have anything to confess?"

"Well, not exactly. I mean, I'm not even Catholic."

"I see. The Church takes converts," Bacon said.

Langston was sure he heard a stifled yawn on the other side of the partition.

"Let us determine if we can expedite matters, shall we? Do you treat your parents with respect?"

"To be honest, my father doesn't think so. But I love them and everything."

"Good. One should never be excessively respectful. It weakens the liver. Where are your kinsmen?"

"My what?"

"The family you spoke of, young man! Please remove the wax from your ears."

"Uh . . . ," Langston replied, trying to think fast. "Far away. *Really* far away. You see, the reason I'm here is . . . there's something I've got to—"

"Are you attentive in your studies?"

"Oh. Yeah. I get straight A's. You know, it's awfully hot in here," Langston said, tugging on his collar.

"A's?"

"Uh . . . I mean, I do really well in school."

"What about science?" Bacon asked more calmly. "Do you take pleasure in it?"

"Does this box have a window?" Langston looked around but didn't see any window. Just airholes. "Huh?" Langston added at last, realizing he hadn't replied to Bacon's last question. "Oh. Sure. Science is my favorite."

"Marvelous! Scientists can be forgiven a multitude of sins."

"Uh . . . actually, I need help with . . . a science experiment. Kind of. Can I meet you somewhere to talk about it?"

CHAPTER XXVII

Dr. Bacon sat down by the fireplace with his cat, Ptolemy, on his lap and sighed wearily. The old man was back at home, had just finished his evening prayers, and was examining some letters he'd received that day. Many were requests for his time, of which he had little to give and none to spare. But one packet caught his immediate attention. The return address was the court of Kublai Khan in Cathay—which in Langston's time was called China.

"Marco Polo!" Bacon exclaimed as he opened the package with delight. "I feared you'd been eaten by tigers, my friend!" He read the letter aloud: "'After much travail I reached the emperor's court sometime last month. The women are *bella*, quite small, but their . . .' Now, Marco," Bacon scolded his friend from afar, "you're writing to a man of the Church!" He skipped ahead in the letter. "'Enclosed please find leaves from the camellia plant, which the people here boil to make a stimulating greenish beverage, and also a recipe for a new delicacy I hope to introduce to *Italia* upon my return.'

"Hmmmm . . . ," Bacon said, withdrawing a large packet of leaves. He sniffed it, then put it aside to examine the recipe curiously. "What say you to this, Ptolemy? 'Pasta.'"

He was interrupted by a knock at the door, and he scooted the cat off his lap. Before the Doctor could ease his old bones out of his chair, another knock followed, louder and more insistent.

"Cease that infernal racket!" he yelled as he reached the door. He opened it.

"Please, Dr. Bacon!" Langston said urgently. "I'm the boy you met at confession today."

With his dark skin and strange clothing, Langston must have looked very odd to Bacon. But the doctor seemed to take no special notice.

"I met a great many boys at confession today," Bacon said curtly. He moved his hand over Langston in the sign of the cross. "*In nomine Patris et Filii et Spiritus Sancti.* You are forgiven. Good night." Bacon started to close the door.

Langston blocked it with his foot. "But . . . I'm the scientist! You said I could—"

Now Bacon appeared to remember their conversation. He opened the door reluctantly.

"In the event that it has escaped your observation, I am a very busy man. I am in the midst of writing an encyclopedia of all knowledge in three volumes: *Opus Majus, Opus Minus, Opus Tertium*. Unless you have some knowledge to convey without which the world will experience some terrible calamity, and on which the entire future of civilization depends, I must insist that you leave."

"But . . . ," Langston said, "that's just it! I do!"

Bacon laughed.

"Please!" Langston pleaded. "You've got to believe—"

But his plea was cut off by the door slamming in his face.

Langston wandered the streets of Oxford town. He was so exhausted he felt like his bones were held together with bubble gum—plus, it was getting dark and he was shivering from the cold. He'd already been in Olde England for hours, and he'd made no progress at all. And there was so little time! He remembered that Mrs. Centauri had told him that in eight days the rare, once-every-888-years alignment of asteroids that had bounced him here would shift. That meant he had only five more days to prevent the invention of gunpowder and save Neely, or he'd never get out of here. Unless . . .

Langston whipped out his pocket calculator and

subtracted 888 from the year he'd left L.A.: 2010.

"1122." Damn! He'd already missed the previous 888-year asteroid synchronicity that allowed time travel. So if he didn't get back home within five days, he'd be stuck here until the *next* synchronicity—in 2010!

Either that, Langston thought ruefully, *or I'll have to wait till 1492 and sail to America with Christopher Columbus! Jeez! I'll be two hundred twenty-eight years old, I'll probably barf on the voyage, and when I finally get home, my family won't even have been born yet.*

Langston thought about his mother. She'd be worried sick about him by now. And what about Mrs. Centauri? As soon as she came home, she'd find his shell and know that he'd used her time machine without her permission. She'd be mad as hell at him!

He tried to put it all out of his mind, but he knew that one way or another, he was in trouble. Humongous trouble.

Langston passed by an inn. Through the open doorway he could see and hear a traveler arguing with the innkeeper over the price of a room. He wouldn't have paid much attention, except that the traveler was accompanied by a beautiful teenage girl whose dark skin glowed like ebony.

"I told you," the innkeeper barked, "I don't make no exceptions!"

"I am the cousin of the lord mayor of Oxford!" the traveler said, puffing out his chest.

"I don't give a brass farthing if you're old King Edward the Longshanks hisself! Two people in a room, you pay double!"

"But this girl is merely a slave!" the traveler said. "You should count her as half a person!"

Langston's stomach turned at the thought of this beautiful girl being held prisoner—and having to sleep in the same room with that sleaze-bucket. He wished desperately that there were something he could do to help her.

The girl turned her head away from the two arguing men, eyes cast down.

"Count her as half a person? Not unless she got half an arse, I won't, you gleeking, fat-kidneyed hornbeast!"

The traveler sputtered in outrage. "You cheeky bastard!" He picked up a tankard of ale from a table and threw it in the innkeeper's face. That started a knock-down, drag-out fight.

The girl saw her opportunity. She ran out into the street—and straight into the arms of the first person she saw.

"Please, kind sir!" she said to Langston. "Hide me!"

Without a moment's hesitation Langston grabbed the girl's hand and they dashed down the street.

A minute later the traveler wiped his bloody nose and glanced around.

"You idiot!" he said to the innkeeper. "She's escaped!"

The man lumbered out of the inn, looking everywhere for his slave girl.

Langston peeked around the corner of a building with a COOPER'S SHOPPE sign on it, spotting the girl's master. He noticed a wine barrel at the side of the building and flung off the lid. It was empty.

"In here!" he said to the girl. "Quick!"

He took her arm and helped her climb into the barrel.

Only a second later her master spun by, looking every which way.

"You! Negro!" the man barked at Langston. "Did you see a Negress come by here?"

"Hab SoSlI' Quch!" Langston replied.

The man stared at him like he was nuts and then ran off.

As soon as Langston was sure the man was gone, he helped the girl out of the barrel.

"I am most grateful to you, sir," she said. "I did not think there were others of my kind here."

"Neither did I," Langston said, feeling like entire regions of his cerebral cortex were blinking out while new ones were lighting up at the sight of her almond-shaped brown eyes, radiant smile, and flawless skin.

"Oh, I smell like wine!" she said, sniffing her clothes, laughing.

"You smell good to me," Langston said.

"What language were you speaking in to my master?"

"Klingon. I told him his mother had a smooth fore-head."

"Kling-on?" she asked. "Where do they speak Klingon?"

"Star Trek."

"Startrek. I have never heard of this country."

"Uh . . . never mind," Langston said with a laugh. "I'm just glad you're safe."

The girl laughed too, though of course she didn't know what was so funny.

Langston glanced around to make sure they weren't being followed. So far, so good. Still . . .

"That creep may come back this way," Langston said. "Where will you go?"

"I have a friend."

"A boy?" Langston didn't know what made him ask this. After all, it was none of his business. But he was very relieved when she replied, "No."

"Good."

The girl blushed and cast her eyes down modestly. They started to walk, hand in hand. Somehow, Langston thought, it seemed perfectly natural to be holding this girl's hand. And they just walked like that in silence for what felt to Langston to be far too short a time, even though it was probably at least half an hour.

"This is where my friend said she would meet me if I could ever escape," the girl said at last, stopping in front of a small stone building.

"Oh," Langston said, disappointed their journey had come to an end.

"A thousand thanks. You have been most kind."

"It was nothing. I . . . I mean, it was something . . . but it was nothing." He could kick himself for sounding like such an idiot.

"I should go inside now, before my master comes back to find me."

"Yes. Of course," Langston said. "Good-bye."

The girl tried to walk away.

"If I am to go, I must have my hand back first," she said, smiling. "It goes with the rest of my body."

"Oh. Of course," he said, quickly letting go of her hand. Now he really felt like an idiot.

"If I can ever help you, you will find me?" she asked.

"Yes! Thank you!" Langston said. "Uh . . . will you stay here?"

She shook her head. "It is too dangerous."

"Then, how will I find you?"

"There will be a way," she said, dashing up the stairs. She took one long look back at him before going in the door.

"Good luck!" Langston said.

Good luck? That's what you say when you're about to take a math quiz—not when you meet the most beautiful girl you've ever seen in your life! Langston worried he might never see her again. And, oh no! He'd never asked her name!

. . . . .

Back in twenty-first-century California, a world-weary cop from the Los Angeles Police Department was standing in the kitchen with Langston's mother, writing out a police report.

"That's all?" the cop said to Langston's mother. She nodded.

"Strangest damn—pardon me, ma'am, I mean *darn*—thing I've seen in twenty years on the force. Okay, ma'am, let me read this all back to you to make sure I got everything right. 'A bottle of window cleaner, a toaster oven, two boxes of oatmeal, a nine-inch aluminum pie pan, a dozen china plates, a waffle iron, a box of strawberry toaster pastries . . .'"

"Honey!" Langston's father called down from the roof. "I found everything! Jeez! Looks like some kind of tornado come through here!"

Langston's shell, of course, had already left the building.

CHAPTER XXVIII

On the moonlit streets of Oxford town Langston stood by the river, watching a man kissing a buxom lady. The couple seemed very busy but not terribly affectionate—almost bored. And somehow Langston thought their relationship was probably a business one, like the deals between the street hookers and johns he'd seen in L.A.

A grimy-faced street urchin who looked to be about fifteen years old approached the man from the back. And while the man was occupied with the lady, the urchin calmly picked his pocket. The boy slipped the money into his cap and put the cap on his head. Then, tipping his cap to the young lady, he walked briskly away. She winked at him when he tipped his cap—apparently an accomplice.

"Hey! You!" Langston called to the boy, chasing him down the street and feeling it was his civic duty to at least say something. He had no idea what kind of behavior was illegal in medieval Britain and what wasn't, but he figured it was probably a pretty safe bet that theft was against the law.

The boy stopped and turned around to face Langston.

Langston stared at the boy, speechless.

"Blimey, guv'nor, what're you gawkin' at? Ain't I got a right same as anybody to make a livin'?"

Langston just kept on staring.

"Uh . . . nothing," Langston replied at last. "You just reminded me of someone . . . I used to know."

For, in fact, the boy was the spitting image of Neely.

"Now, there's a good one! You thinkin' you seen me before. Not unless you been in Newgate Prison, mate!"

The boy came closer to Langston and stared at him, too. He touched Langston's face, then examined his own finger. Langston jerked back.

"Blimey!" the boy said. "Your color don't come off, now, do it? You look like someone left you roastin' o'er a fire too long, guv'nor!"

Langston didn't like it, but he had to give the kid credit for cojones.

The boy could see Langston was a little annoyed.

"I don't mean nothin' by it. It's just me way," the boy said, extending his hand. "Niles, at your service. Pleased to make yer 'quaintance." He gave Langston a little tip of his cap.

Langston shook his hand. "I'm Langston. A lot of people look like me where I come from."

118

"'eaven?"

"Heaven! No," Langston said. "Why'd you think that?"

"Well, blimey, just 'cause I ain't been to school don't mean I can't bloody read!"

Niles pointed to Langston's jacket.

"Oh, Anaheim Angels!" Langston said. "That's just a baseball team!"

"What's that you say?"

"Uh . . . I think it would take too long to explain."

Niles shrugged, took off his cap, and started counting the stolen coins. "Quite a 'aul for a day's work, now, ain't it!"

"Didn't your folks teach you that's wrong?"

"Wrong?" Niles asked, sounding insulted. He pointed back to the prostitute still occupying the robbed man's attention. "I split the money wi'er fair an' square, right down the middle, I does!"

He grabbed Langston in a choke hold.

"You ain't callin' me a crook, now, are ya, mate?"

Langston could barely breathe. He choked out a reply. "No . . . er . . . course not."

Niles released him and laughed.

"Besides," Niles said, "I ain't got none."

"No family? That's too bad."

"Too bad? Me life improved consid'rable when me old man died. Beat me wivin an inch o' me life, 'e did.

'Cept, o' course, when 'e 'ad too much ale. Then 'e whacked me wivin a quarter inch!"

Langston looked at him sympathetically, but Niles wasn't the sort to feel sorry for himself. In fact, he seemed to be enjoying himself immensely.

"You have any place to sleep?"

"Sure I does," Niles said, yawning. "I'm pretty knackered meself." He looked around, pointing to various areas of the street.

"Let's see. There's a pile o' offal there that looks invitin'. And that pig wagon wiv the 'ay piled in it . . ."

"Neither do I," Langston said with a sigh.

"And if none of them suits me fancy, there's always Father Bacon's lordly 'stablishment."

"You know Dr. Bacon?" Langston exclaimed.

"Crikey! Don't bite me arm off!" Niles said. "Sure, the old man an' I is the closest of 'quaintances, we is. 'E give me a bob now an' then. . . ."

"Niles—I need you to do me a favor. . . ."

CHAPTER XXIX

Dr. Bacon was asleep, dreaming of a design for a flying machine. His plans were almost done—all that remained was to devise a method of flexing the machine's wings to adjust its path during flight.

And then an infernal knocking woke him! Another great invention lost to humanity! A second round of knocking finally rousted Dr. Bacon out of bed.

"I'm coming, you impertinent, clay-brained clot pole!"

Dr. Bacon had no idea who would be bothering him at this ungodly hour of the night. But whoever he was, Bacon decided, the description would certainly apply.

"'Ello, Father," Niles said cheerfully as Bacon opened the door.

"*You* again!" Bacon rolled his eyes skyward. "Oh, heavenly Father, what terrible sin have I committed to earn your despisement?" He turned back to Niles, waving his hands as though shooing away flies.

"Depart! Withdraw! Do . . . whatever you do when you're not tormenting me!"

Langston, who was hiding in the shadows behind Niles, whispered in the Cockney kid's ear, "I thought you said he likes you!"

"Shut up!"

"What?" Bacon said. "How dare you!"

"Oh, I didn't mean you, Father," Niles said quickly. "I—I was talkin' wiv the devil, who's always whisperin' temptation in me ear."

"Well—*go* to him, then!" Bacon said, starting to slam the door.

Having considerable practice at such things, Niles stuck his foot in the door to block it from closing.

"Ow! Now, Father, is that any way to treat one of your most deservin' poor?"

"Poor! Niles, with the money I've given you in just the past fortnight, you could set yourself up at Windsor Castle!"

"Maligned, that's what I is!" Niles said with a moan. "I come 'ere to do you a good turn—mind, wivout a jot in it for me—an' this is the thanks me gets!"

"Good turn?"

"I brung you a friend o' mine. 'E's honest an' true, make no mistake. An' the most pious bloke in jolly old England! Prays mornin', noon, an' night!"

"Morning, noon, and night?" Langston whispered in his ear.

"Shhh!" Niles whispered back, swatting behind him. "Don't bother me while I'm embellishin'!"

Niles turned his attention back to Bacon. "Bright as a new penny, 'e is. Just down on 'is luck is all. 'E's not used to sleepin' on the street like I is."

Niles pulled his new friend into view.

"'Is name's Langston. Will you let 'im stay the night, Father? Just this once?"

"No!"

"I'll go now an' I won't beg a coin off you for a whole week?"

This idea seemed to appeal to Bacon. "You swear?"

"On me mum's grave."

"Two weeks," Bacon said.

"But, Father—you're me best customer!"

"Niles . . . ," Bacon warned, "that's my best offer. 'Tyke it or lyve it,' as you might say."

"Well . . ." Niles hesitated. He looked at Langston, whose eyes sent out an appeal to him. Niles reached to shake Bacon's hand.

"Deal," Niles agreed.

And with that, he tipped his cap and sauntered away, leaving Langston alone with Dr. Bacon.

· · · · ·

Mrs. Centauri and Alpha had made an emergency trip to the dentist all the way in downtown Los Angeles on

Saturday morning because Alpha had knocked out a tooth after falling out of bed. Luckily, Alpha was okay and the dentist had said her tooth was just a baby one that would have fallen out eventually anyway. As a reward for not crying when the dentist examined her, Mrs. Centauri had taken Alpha to the Natural History Museum to see the dinosaurs and then out to dinner at a restaurant where all the waiters were dressed up like tyrannosaurs and danced in a conga line.

"Mom," Alpha said as they walked in the front door later that night, "does the tooth fairy pay for teeth that get knocked out? Or only ones that fall out the way they're supposed to?"

"Either way, Al. I think she's an equal-opportunity fairy," Mrs. Centauri replied, carrying in the milk bottles. "Why don't you put your tooth under your pillow when you go to bed and see if anything happens?"

Mrs. Centauri went into the observatory to check a chart of natural satellites. On her way through the living room she noticed a mirror propped up near the iridium laser machine.

That's funny, she thought—she couldn't remember having put a mirror there. But it *did* look just like an old one she kept stored in the closet. And the cleaning lady had come by, so maybe she'd moved it. Mrs. Centauri didn't think any more about it.

Alpha sat down at Mrs. Centauri's computer in the

living room and looked at the monitor. She read the words off the window open in front of her.

"'Meet the remarkable Roger Bacon, one of the world's first scientists, who was hundreds of years ahead of his time. . . .' Mom! Have you been messing around with my encyclopedia again? I was reading about *Stegosaurus,* and you lost my place!"

"Not now, please, honey!" Mrs. Centauri called back. "It's way past your bedtime, and I'm trying to figure out the orbital period of Mars's moon Deimos."

Alpha just shrugged and clicked the computer window closed.

CHAPTER XXX

"You've got to believe me!" Langston pleaded.

For the past half hour he had been trying to explain things to Dr. Bacon, but he seemed to be getting nowhere.

Bacon crossed his arms and looked stern.

"You say that my research will one day be used to create terrible weapons of destruction that will cause tens of millions of deaths on battlefields and the streets of towns and cities. You say these weapons will shatter bone and flesh and cause massive explosions—and fire will rain from the skies. You say you know this because you are from the future and so can prophesy future events."

"Yes!" Langston said, relieved that he was finally getting through to the old man.

"I will take your leave and return after a brief interval," Bacon said, and without another word he stepped out his door and onto the dark street.

"Fatima! Fatima!" he called, going around the corner.

Meanwhile, Ptolemy rubbed himself against Langston's jeans and purred. Langston bent over to pet him.

"What's your name, fuzzball?"

Then the cat circled the room, as if urging Langston to follow, jumping on and off of the crude, simple furniture. Langston took this opportunity to look around. Dr. Bacon's house was really more of a scientific laboratory than a home, with lots of colored liquids bubbling in glass bottles and test tubes, glass lenses of various shapes and sizes, a brass telescope on a stand, a celestial globe, and labeled sacks of chemical powders, and there was a slight rotten-egg smell of sulfur in the air. The shelves were lined with so many books—most of them looked to be quite ancient— that they tilted precariously under the weight. And on one corner of a table, next to a straw bed, was what looked like a primitive pair of reading spectacles.

Langston picked up a book from Dr. Bacon's table. It was open, with a quill pen resting across the pages. He knew it wasn't right to look at other people's stuff without their permission, but his curiosity got the better of him. The book had lots of handwritten notes in it, in some sort of code—and drawings, including one that looked like a winged flying machine! Was it the book that Dr. Bacon was writing?

A moment later Langston heard the door open, so he put the book down quickly, jumped away from the table, and shoved his hands in his pockets. Dr. Bacon had returned with a pitiable, wild-eyed woman. Her eyes glittered like blue marbles, and her spiky, gray-streaked hair went in a million different directions. When she saw Langston, the woman trembled, backing away and cowering like a child. Dr. Bacon gently took her hand and led her over to Langston.

"Don't be frightened, my dear," he said. "Tell the young lad what you know."

"We'll all burn, I say! Burn like swine from a cloud of dust that bursts from small entities holding all the power of the cosmos and falls like black rain from the devil. The apocalypse! The apocalypse is coming, I tell you!"

Suddenly the woman grabbed Langston by the shoulders, her eyes bulging in excitement. He stood there, frozen with fear and disgust.

The woman dissolved into hysterical laughter. Dr. Bacon pried the woman's hands off of Langston. Langston quickly recovered his senses—and his voice.

"What she said—that sounds like the atomic bomb!"

"Thank you, Fatima," Bacon said kindly to the woman. He handed her a few coins, and she laughed again. Then she ran from the room and out the door.

"They kept her chained to a wall until I intervened to stop it," Bacon said to Langston.

"I know . . . I know I must sound crazy like her! But what I've been telling you is true!"

Dr. Bacon blew out a candle, climbed into the straw bed, and pulled a crude blanket over himself.

"If I do not awaken in time for your departure on the morrow, have a pleasant journey."

"But . . ."

Langston felt utterly powerless. Then he got an idea. He took his calculator out of his shirt pocket and pressed the ON button.

"Give me a multiplication problem," Langston said. "Go ahead! A hard one."

Dr. Bacon was already half asleep. "Four million three thousand ninety-seven times nine," he muttered.

Langston did the sum on his calculator in less than three seconds.

"Thirty-six million twenty-seven thousand eight hundred seventy-three," Langston announced.

"Correct," Bacon replied. "Bravo. Of course, I could calculate to fourteen decimal places without the aid of quill and parchment by the time I was four."

"But—look!" Langston said, holding out the calculator so Bacon could see it. "I did it on a machine! From the twenty-first century!"

"Ducky," Bacon said, eyes closed, yawning. "Good night . . ."

And the slow, steady beat of his breathing told Langston that Dr. Bacon was already fast asleep.

Langston sighed with frustration. *It's hopeless!* he thought. *This guy will never believe me! Well, might as well get some sleep too.* He hadn't realized it before now, but he had never been so tired in his life.

Langston lay down on some straw in the corner—Ptolemy was already snoozing blissfully in the only comfortable chair—and put his contact lenses in their plastic container in his pocket. Langston immediately fell into a deep slumber, as if he hadn't slept in centuries.

· · · · ·

Back in L.A., Langston's father was in his repair shop, lying on his back under a Lexus, fixing the axle. He'd gotten an emergency call that night from an anxious young family whose car had broken down on the way to Disneyland. He had arranged to have their Lexus towed to his shop, and they had promised to pay him double if he could get them back on the road in under two hours.

The owners of the car were standing nearby, passing the time by teaching their baby to talk. Langston's shell was listening dumbly to what the husband was saying.

"Da-da," the young man said to the baby. "Let's hear you say Da-da, Millicent. Can you do that for Daddy? Say, 'Yes, Da-da. Yes, Da-da.'" The man made silly faces. "Well then, say, 'No, Daddy.' Can you at least do that?" He turned to his wife, exasperated. "She's not doing it, honey. I swear she did it this morning. . . ."

"Give me a wrench," Langston's father said to his son's shell.

The shell handed him something.

"Not a screwdriver! A wrench!"

The shell handed him a can of soda.

"Skip it!" Langston's father growled. "I'll get it myself."

Langston's father slid out from under the car. He searched through a toolbox.

"You know, your ma and I have noticed you been actin' . . . different lately. Maybe you still don't know a wrench from a screwdriver, but in general you been real cooperative."

"Yes, Da-da," the shell said.

"Are you sassing me?"

"No, Daddy."

"Real cooperative," Langston's father continued. "I mean, we like it. Like your attitude. Your mama says you been minding her real good today."

Then Langston's father did something he hadn't done in years. He patted him—or the boy who looked like him—on the shoulder.

"Keep up the good work, son."

CHAPTER XXXI

Rome, Italy—January 17, 1278

Pope Clement IV sat on his great thronelike chair in the Lateran Palace, counting coins into a parchment pouch addressed to a certain teacher of science at Oxford University. The pope was weak in body but strong in moral courage and spirit.

When the door opened suddenly, the pope quickly hid the pouch under his robes.

Jerome of Ascoli entered, kneeled, and kissed the pope's ring.

"Well?" the pope demanded. "Did you find out who is responsible for the destruction of Roger Bacon's laboratory?"

"No, Your Holiness," Jerome responded. "Father Bacon has many enemies."

"And one friend! His is the greatest mind of the century. As long as I am pope, Roger Bacon will be permitted to teach and conduct his experiments without interference from the Church." The pope stared pointedly at Jerome. "Is that clear, Brother Jerome?"

Jerome hid his discomfort well, but the pope had no illusions about him.

"Yes, Your Holiness," Jerome replied, bowing his head. "If it please Your Holiness, have you ever wondered how a friar who has taken a vow of poverty obtained the money to buy all those pretty glass bottles and tubes for his experiments?"

The pope glared at him. "No. I don't wonder!"

The pope's hand shifted over the pouch under his robes. Jerome became suspicious but said nothing.

"Now, get out!" the pope demanded. "I need to prepare for mass."

· · · · ·

When he woke up, it took Langston a few seconds to remember where he was.

Dr. Bacon was sitting at the table, writing in a book with fierce concentration and at a furious pace. Langston approached quietly, looking over the old man's shoulder. From time to time Dr. Bacon would stop writing to rub a needle against a small stone, then float the needle on a tiny wooden raft in a tray of water.

"What are you working on?" Langston asked.

"Yiiihhh!" Bacon was so startled he almost leaped

out of his chair. The quill pen went flying and the ink spilled on the table. "Zounds! My encyclopedia!"

Frantic, Bacon checked to make sure no ink had spilled on the book. Fortunately there was no damage. Langston helped him sop up the ink with some woolen rags.

"Sorry," he said to Dr. Bacon. Bacon glared at him with a ferocity that said more than words, then went back to his experiment with the needle and the stone.

"Magnetism," the doctor said at last. "I have discovered that when I rub a thin iron needle with a lodestone and suspend the needle in a liquid medium by floating it on a bit of cork bark so that it may spin freely, it points in the general direction of the nautical star."

"You've invented the compass!"

Puzzled, Bacon looked at him, then shrugged. "Once I complete my encyclopedia and the pope receives it, the world will be lifted up out of the darkness of ignorance! Science will become the common knowledge of the masses."

"Is your formula for gunpowder in that book?" Langston asked, worried.

"My formula for what?"

"Oh. Right. You don't know what guns are. Uh . . . the powder that can explode."

"Ah! My marvelous Black Powder. No, it won't be in my encyclopedia. I wrote it in a secret—hold, young man! How do *you* know of this?"

"I told you," Langston replied. "I'm from the future."

"Balderdash!" Bacon started writing again. Langston was frustrated by the old man's stubbornness. He leaned over to get a better look at something Bacon was writing. Tired of trying to read Bacon's tiny scrawl, he took his contact lens case out of his pocket. Unfortunately there was no place to clean the lenses. *The water here has to be loaded with crap*, Langston thought, so he simply rubbed spit on a lens, leaned his head back, and . . .

"Good Lord!" Bacon said. "What are you doing to your eye?"

"Putting in contacts. Er . . . lenses. So I can see better. They go on my eyeballs."

Bacon grabbed Langston's hands. "I insist you cease this self-mutilation at once!"

"They won't hurt me. Look . . ."

Langston demonstrated. He put a lens in each eye, then popped them out again and handed the lenses to Bacon.

Bacon examined them skeptically, then put a lens under what looked like a primitive microscope.

"Hmmm . . . ," Bacon said. "Convex. Several diopters of correction."

"Go ahead," Langston said. "Try them."

Bacon would never turn down an experiment in the

interest of science. Steeling himself, he put the contacts in his own eyes.

"Your prescription—I mean, the shape of your eyeballs—may not be the same as mine," Langston said.

Bacon picked up his book and looked at a page. "I— I can read like a man of twenty! These are even better than those spectacles I invented. You're another Merlin, boy!"

"But I didn't *invent* them. I told you, I'm from the fu—"

"Future . . . ," Bacon mused, quietly amazed. In a matter of seconds his whole attitude toward Langston did a complete reversal. "Remarkable! But . . . how?"

"Well, it's sort of like I'm a moving picture—made of light—and I came here on a laser. That's a really strong beam of light that can travel great distances."

Bacon thought this over. "Yes, yes. Light moves rapidly and persists. I could see how such a thing could be. Yes!"

He rapidly scribbled down some notes in his book.

"I need an apprentice," Bacon said. "An eager young mind! Someone to whom I can transfer my knowledge and to assist me in finishing my *Opus Tertium*. Will you?"

"Uh . . . sure. But to tell you the truth, I can't stick around here very long."

Bacon, oblivious to anything but Langston's affirmative reply, immediately started clearing off a place at the cluttered table for Langston to work.

"It's kind of complicated," Langston continued.

"But in four days the asteroids that bounced me here are gonna move. And they won't be in that position again for another eight hundred eighty-eight—"

Bacon handed him a daunting stack of parchment papers. "I want you to transcribe the records of these experiments. . . ."

Bacon sat down, quill pen in hand, and added: "And tell me *all about the future*. . . ."

"Well, that's the whole story," Langston told Dr. Bacon, finishing his summary. "Seven hundred years in a nutshell."

"Amazing!" Bacon said. "Nearly everything I predicted will come true! But what took them such an extraordinary amount of time?"

"Beats me," Langston said with a shrug. "I guess everyone was too busy shooting one another."

Langston examined a book Dr. Bacon had handed him.

"So this is it . . . the formula for gunpowder," Langston said, awed and horrified at the same time. "The whole thing started right here."

"The formula is in anagrams," said Bacon. "That means I've arranged the letters in each word out of sequence to make it difficult for the casual observer to decipher. Six parts powder of the petral stone, five of young willow charcoal, five of sulfur. Here's a sample."

Bacon reached in the pocket of his habit, removed a small glass vial, and handed it to him. Langston pulled out the stopper, sniffed at the acrid powder, wrinkling his nose, then handed it back.

The old man moved behind a screen and took off his robes. He climbed into a big wooden tub.

"Pour me a bath," he ordered brusquely. "The buckets are by the fire." *Well,* Langston thought ruefully as he got the buckets, *I guess filling bathtubs is what apprentices do.*

Turning his head aside so he wouldn't offend Bacon's modesty, Langston slowly poured a bucket of hot water into the tub.

"By Jove!" Bacon said from his bath. "It will be a good thing indeed for the common people when— what did you call them?—*guns* are invented."

Langston dumped a second bucket into the tub, all at once.

"Zounds!" Bacon roared. "It's too hot!"

"It'll be a *good* thing?" Langston said angrily. "A gun killed my best friend!"

There was a long pause.

"I am sorry," Bacon said, sounding genuinely sympathetic. "You did not speak to me of this."

"I . . . I know," Langston said. "I didn't want you to think that this was all about me, that the only reason I came here was to try to save my friend."

"Well—isn't it?"

Langston thought a moment.

"Yes," he admitted. "At least, mostly."

"The great Greek philosopher Diogenes searched in vain all his life for an honest man," Bacon said thoughtfully. "He would have found one today—in you. You are here to help a friend. There is no shame in that. You want me to destroy my formula for Black Powder, so that it will be lost to history. I understand. But I regret to say . . . I cannot do what you ask."

Langston groaned.

"Come with me," Bacon said, getting out of the tub, dressing quickly, and heading for the door. "I have something to show you that perhaps may help you to understand."

CHAPTER XXXII

Dr. Bacon was taking Langston on a guided tour of peasant squalor in medieval Oxford. Ringing a bell, a ragged leper with a terribly disfigured face approached them. His nose looked half chewed away, as if rats had nibbled on it—but it was really from the disease of leprosy. As the leper rang his bell, people quickly and fearfully cleared his path.

"The king's law requires that all lepers ring a bell to warn people of their approach," Dr. Bacon explained.

Peasants, many of whom appeared to know the good doctor, mobbed him, begging for coins or food. He gave a penny to a woman carrying a baby that looked like it had smallpox on its face.

"Bless you, Father," the woman said, weeping with gratitude.

As they continued, Bacon pointed out a patch of grayish-green land. Langston could see peasants laboring in the fields, doing the backbreaking work of clearing away dead weeds and wheat stalks—probably left over from last year's harvest. The workers looked just like the medieval harvesters in an old painting by a dude named Brueghel that Langston had seen in a book at school. But several of these real guys were being whipped by an overseer when they didn't work fast enough to suit him.

"Serfs," Bacon said soberly.

"Like slaves," Langston said.

Bacon pointed to the overseer. "And that's the beadle. He keeps them in line."

"He's worse than the cops who beat up kids in L.A.! Why are you showing me this?"

Bacon stretched his arm toward a castle looming in the distance. "The lord of the manor owns these people. Their sticks and hoes could never break down those stone walls. As long as the castles stand, the poor of England will never be free! But there is one thing that could make those walls come tumbling down—like Joshua blowing his trumpet to bring down the walls of Jericho."

Feeling defeated, Langston knew what Dr. Bacon meant. "Guns," he said.

When they returned to Bacon's house, Langston warmed his cold hands near the fire and looked out the window at the passing scene of life. So many ordinary people, young and old, living in ignorance and slavery. *Maybe Dr. Bacon is right,* Langston thought. If guns would set all these poor people free, who was he to stand in the way of progress? Maybe freedom was more important than the life of one boy—even if he *was* Langston's best friend. Maybe freedom was even more important than all the millions of people who had died from guns. Where would the human race be if things stayed stuck in medieval times, people tilling the fields for their masters and just barely getting by, believing in witches, with nobody able to vote and hardly anybody knowing how to read or write?

Langston watched a couple of teenage boys playing what looked like a primitive version of stickball or cricket. They were horsing around together—the way boys had done for hundreds of years before this and would forever after.

Langston watched the boys laughing together. And suddenly he felt that what he was seeing was worth more than all the freedom in the world. That love and friendship—the ties that linked you to everybody you cared about—were more important than the circumstances you lived in. Here were a couple of poor kids who probably owned nothing more than the filthy clothes on their backs. But they were friends, and that's what really mattered. What good was freedom if your best friend wasn't there to share it with you? What good was progress if it meant going forward alone?

What good was a game of stickball without a guy you could count on to rag on you about your lousy swing?

Langston's mind was made up. He rose from his chair, picked up Dr. Bacon's book containing the formula for gunpowder, and brought it to him.

"Burn it," he said. "Please, Dr. Bacon! Just one page of it."

Bacon pushed his spectacles down on his nose and looked up at Langston. "For the last time: No!"

"You want there to be guns," Langston snapped back, strong and defiant, "because you want the peasants to fight for their freedom—and you love these people, like, as a group. You've got all the sympathy in the world for them! As long as they don't get too close. But what about having feelings for *one* person? Maybe you can't understand how I feel because you don't know what it means to lose somebody you love. Maybe you've never cared about anybody at all!"

For once Dr. Bacon was dumbstruck.

"Well? Have you?"

Bacon still didn't reply.

Langston knew he'd won this round. But when he saw the deeply pained look on Dr. Bacon's face, he was almost sorry he had.

CHAPTER XXXIII

Langston was wandering the streets of Oxford town looking for Niles. He finally found him performing a medieval version of the modern street scam three-card monte. The gathered crowd watched Niles with rapt attention as he shuffled the cards around on a wooden box faster than their eyes could follow.

"Round an' round the queenie goes, an' where she stops, nobody knows!" Niles said.

Over and over again a shill in the crowd—Niles's accomplice—guessed the right card, but the innocent dupes bet the wrong one. *Time marches on, but people never change,* Langston thought, remembering all the suckers he'd seen taken in by this con game on the streets of L.A.

Niles was really raking in the dough.

"'Ello, mate," Niles called, winking at Langston. "An honest day's pay for an honest day's work."

Langston gave him a disapproving look.

"Game's over, ladies an' gents," Niles announced. "It was a pleasure taking—uh . . . *meeting* you."

Niles stuffed the money under his cap and gathered up his playing cards. The boys walked along as Niles practiced card tricks.

"Niles, you know Dr. Bacon better than I do," Langston said. "If you wanted to talk him into something, how would you do it?"

"Tryin' to pry a few bob out of 'im, eh, mate?"

"No. Nothing like that."

"When I'm tryin' to persuade a bloke to me way of thinkin', I ask meself, 'Now, what sort of bloke is 'e?' I speak 'is language. Is 'e a farmer? Then, I talk cows. A tavern keeper? I talk ale."

"Dr. Bacon is a scientist," Langston said.

"Zactly. Then, I'd talk to 'im like one. What do a scientist need for convincin'?"

Langston considered.

"An experiment," he said at last. "Evidence."

"Dr. Bacon won't believe nothin' 'e can't see"— Niles made a playing card disappear and reappear from behind Langston's ear—"wiv 'is own eyes!"

"With his own eyes . . . ," Langston repeated, getting an idea. "That's it! Niles, I have to go . . . away for about a day. I need you to do something for me while I'm gone."

"You could not have chosen a more inopportune moment!" Bacon complained when Langston spoke with him that evening during dinner.

"I know I promised to help you finish the encyclopedia, but I'll only be away one day. What difference could just a day make?"

"Time is of the essence! The pope is not a young man. If my work doesn't reach him before he passes away, Brother Jerome will see to it that it never reaches the light of day."

"Brother Jerome?"

"Jerome of Ascoli." He pointed to Langston's plate. "Eat your turnips. He's the general of my Franciscan order and a toothache of a man. He's next in line to be pope."

Dr. Bacon's cat jumped on the table.

"Ptolemy! You have better manners than that!" Bacon said, lifting the cat to the floor. He turned back to Langston. "There is a boat departing for Rome on the morrow. If my encyclopedia isn't on it, there may not be another one to Italy for three months!"

"Everything'll be okay—you'll get it done in time. Look—I even brought someone to help you with your work while I'm away. . . ."

Langston got up to bring Niles into the room from outside, where he had been waiting, ear pressed to the door. Niles waved hello to Dr. Bacon, then without invitation dived right into the food on the table, stuffing himself.

"Saints preserve us," Bacon said, shaking his head.

Langston excused himself from the table and went outside. He looked left and right down the dark street to make sure no one was watching, then pressed the Solo Voyager Earth Return button on his laser remote control device. A green beam of laser light ping-ponged across the asteroid belt like a lightning bolt, then carried Langston off into space.

After being buffeted by the fiery explosion of gas and charged particles from a solar storm, Langston waved a quick, passing hello to his holographic twin 732 light-years out in space, then bounced right back into Mrs. Centauri's observatory—all in the blink of an eye.

It was already Monday morning in Los Angeles. Langston figured that the solar storm he'd passed through must have temporarily disrupted the programming in his laser remote control, dropping him into L.A. a few hours later than he'd expected. He wouldn't have much time.

Luckily, Mrs. Centauri and Alpha were out. So were Sirius 1 and 2. *Maybe the dogs are out for a walk with Mrs. Centauri's cleaning lady,* Langston thought, noticing their leashes were gone from the coatrack and a plugged-in vacuum cleaner was left in the middle of the rug. *I guess even holographic dogs need to go for a poop.*

He looked at the calendar on Mrs. Centauri's desk. Monday, January 18. Martin Luther King Jr. Day! The day of Banneker's big basketball game against Christopher

Columbus High! With all the excitement lately he'd totally forgotten about it—though he wasn't really missing anything, since all Coach ever let him do was warm the bench.

Most of Banneker High would be closed for the holiday, and anyone there would be too busy watching the game to notice what he'd be up to—so that was good news.

Langston looked at his watch—9:02. If he could just get a ride in a hurry, he'd arrive at school while the game was still going on.

Langston was in such a rush to get going that he didn't even notice his shell was missing.

He picked up the phone, got a number from voice-activated directory assistance, and was connected.

The phone on the other end rang four times, and then a message machine picked up.

"This is Jerry the Milkman at Strawberry Fields Farms—drink fresh milk and rock your world, baby! The cows and I are out moooovin' and groovin', so lay a message on us at the beep, and we'll get back to you."

Beep! Beep! Beep! Screech!

"Is this thing on? Uh . . . listen, man, this is Langston. The kid from Mrs. Centauri's who bummed a ride off of you? I was wondering if you could do me a favor and pick me up at her house when you get this, I'm late for the big game. Thanks."

During their trip down from the mountain Jerry the milkman asked what seemed to Langston to be some pretty crazy questions about how Langston had managed to get back to Mrs. Centauri's, when Jerry had just seen him walking down from the mountain there the day before. Langston was so confused all he could do was try to change the subject—until the milkman finally dropped him off at the rear entrance to Benjamin Banneker High.

Langston sneaked past the noisy gym and heard some Banneker cheerleaders through the door.

"Banneker Blazers! We're amazers!" they chanted.

Jeez! Langston thought. *Those dweebs gotta get a better cheer.*

Langston dashed down the deserted hallway and tried the door to the A/V office. *Rats!* Locked.

Just then he spotted the A/V office assistant coming out of the boys' bathroom.

"Miguel—*mi compadre!*" Langston said, jogging up to him with a forced smile and putting an arm around the tenth-grader's shoulders.

"Uh-oh," Miguel said. "He's calling me *compadre* again. Must mean he wants something."

"All right, all right. Look, I just need you to unlock the A/V office for me."

"Man, don't bug me now, we're losing the game, I haven't slept in two days, and I'm going home! Besides, you know kids aren't allowed in the A/V." Miguel started walking away.

"It'll only take a few minutes!" Langston pleaded, trotting after him. "All you gotta do is open that door and let me borrow a portable DVD player with a built-in screen for a few days. I'll need some history DVDs—and oh yeah, I gotta use the computer editing equipment too."

"Yeah, that sounds great," Miguel replied sarcastically. "We break into the A/V office, and I let you walk out of here with a few thousand dollars' worth of school equipment. Why don't we rob friggin' MTV Studios while we're at it?"

"Please—I'm in a hurry! We won't really have to *break* in—you've got the key. And I promise I'll return everything before anyone notices they're missing."

Miguel just shook his head sleepily and headed for the exit.

Suddenly Langston got an inspiration. He ran after Miguel.

"How are you doing in science class?"

"Huh? *Realmente* lousy. Been crammin' all weekend for a test I'm gonna flunk anyway. Why?"

"I'll tutor you for nothing. You'll be acing your science tests in six weeks, or I'll buy you two tickets to see Bettina Marquez sing at the Hollywood Bowl."

"Bettina the Babe, huh? You drive a hard bargain, man. Hey, how 'bout we just skip the science part and you get me those tickets?"

Langston shook his head. "Nope."

Miguel sighed and thought it over.

"Trato hecho," he said at last. Langston looked puzzled.

"That means you got a deal, *amigo.* Just zip your lip about all this, okay?"

"Thanks! I won't tell."

"And I better trade you Spanish lessons for science. What century you livin' in, man? You want to live in this world, you better learn more Spanish."

Moments later Langston was busy editing digital images on a computer in the school's editing room.

"Here's a bunch more of them, *amigo.*" An exhausted Miguel sneaked a precariously balanced stack of DVDs into the editing room and set them down on the table next to Langston. *"D-Day: Omaha Beach, Vietnam Odyssey,"* he read some titles off the labels and yawned. *"Qué pasa?* You doing some kind of book report for your history teacher?"

"Uh . . . you might say that," Langston replied. But when he turned around a minute later, Miguel was already fast asleep on a chair.

· · · · ·

Meanwhile, the big championship basketball game was in its fourth quarter. The home team was trailing by twenty points.

Suddenly the ref blew his whistle. The Blazers' number seven, "Gross-out" Gary Dunwoodie, got called out of the game on a foul when he kicked a player from Christopher Columbus High in the shin. Gary shuffled off the court sullenly, picking his nose. The Banneker Blazers had lost their best point guard!

Desperate, their coach turned to a tall kid who had just walked into the gym wearing a big zero on his basketball jersey. The kid had his jersey on backward—and was sitting alone on the Blazers' bench staring into space.

"All right," Coach said, dragging number zero to his feet. "I guess we ain't got a choice. Get in there—and God help us."

The ref started the clock again. One of the other Blazers passed the ball to number zero, who caught the ball and then just stood there doing nothing.

"Pass! Pass, you putz! *Jeez!*"

A Columbus High player snatched the ball from number zero, and the visiting team scored three times in less than a minute. The Blazers were twenty-six points behind!

Curses flew from the coach's mouth that would have made a gangsta rapper blush. Then: "Time out!"

He stomped over to number zero. "The idea of the game is you dribble, shoot, or pass. Get it, Davis? Dribble, shoot, or pass!"

"Yes, Daddy," Langston's shell replied.

"None of your lip, wise guy! You see that basket? Now, I want to see you put that damn ball in there fifty times—or you'll have to answer to me, you hear?"

The coach signaled the ref, who tossed the ball back into play and blew his whistle.

Langston's shell caught the ball and robotically fired it at the basket. *Swoosh!* And then again and again—and again! *Swoosh, swoosh!* Every time he scored, the Columbus team got the ball out of bounds on the endline and whipped it downcourt toward one of their players. But the shell kept stealing the inbound pass and draining it, while his teammates just stood there, jaws dropping. Twenty points. *Swoosh!* He was unstoppable! Thirty. Sixty! A hundred! The crowd was on its feet, cheering.

After scoring fifty times, Langston's shell suddenly headed for the door—carrying the basketball.

"Wait! Where are you going?" Coach shouted.

Bzzzzz! The final buzzer. The Banneker Blazers were the new high school basketball champions of L.A.!

Ecstatic Blazers and cheering fans rushed the coach, quickly burying him under a mound of bodies.

"You're a genius, kid!" Coach shouted from under the pile. "Come back, Davis! We'll get you a million dollars in sneaker endorsements!"

But the shell just opened the door and stepped out into the hallway.

WHAM!

"Hey! Don't you even say excuse me?" Langston said, getting up off the floor and examining the DVD player to make sure it wasn't damaged. Then he got a good look at who had knocked him down.

"Holy moly, it's you!" Langston gasped, staring right into the glazed-over eyes of his identical twin.

Langston did a quick calculation. He figured there was good news and bad news. The good news was that if his shell was running around loose in school instead of hanging out at Mrs. Centauri's place, then she probably had no idea Langston had hijacked her time machine.

The bad news was that there were *two* Langstons running around Benjamin Banneker High.

"Quick!" Langston said, looping his belt through the DVD player's holder to free up his hands, then grabbing his shell by the elbow. "Come with me!"

He tried to drag the shell along, but it was like trying to move a stubborn mule. Langston looked around frantically for some place to hide him, but all the classrooms were locked. Then he took a peek around the corner and saw two people he knew coming down the hall.

Ohmigod. Mrs. Centauri! With Alpha!

It was too late to escape. Langston grabbed the basketball from his shell just as Mrs. Centauri and Alpha rounded the corner. He used the ball to cover his own face.

"Langston!" Mrs. Centauri said, addressing the shell. "What are you doing standing out here? I was just showing Alpha our bio lab's hamster. We left the gym in the third quarter—that game's a real snoozer!"

The shell just stared at her blankly.

"Yeah, I know exactly how you feel. Missed seeing you in class last Friday, kiddo. You playing hooky? Don't worry, I understand . . . ," she said sympathetically, putting her hand on the shell's shoulder. "You're still feeling bad about Neely. I've never seen you look so spaced out."

She pointed to the real Langston, who had the basketball covering up his face. "Who's your shy friend?"

"I'm Rajeed," the original Langston said in a deep voice with a weird accent. "I'm the new exchange student from Ethiopia."

"Great! Welcome to America!" Mrs. Centauri said. "Why don't you come visit my class when you're feeling a little . . . uh . . . braver." She turned back to the shell.

"Langston, you won't miss this Friday's class, will you?"

"No, Daddy," the shell said.

"Very funny," Mrs. Centauri said drily. "Well, at least you haven't lost your sense of humor." She looked toward the gym. "What's all that noise in there?" She turned back to Langston. "Gotta run back to the game, kiddo. Remember: Don't miss my next class. We're going to study the constellation Gemini, the twins!"

Mrs. Centauri took off down the hall, but Alpha lingered. Suddenly the girl leaped up and knocked the basketball away from Langston.

"Ooooooh," she said, staring at him and the shell in wonder. Then she chanted in a singsong voice, "Langston's got a *se*-cret! Langston's got a *se*-cret!"

Langston snatched the basketball back, knelt down, and grabbed her arm.

"Ow!"

"Alpha! *Please!* I'll do anything! Just don't tell anyone!"

Alpha was a smart little girl. She realized she'd never been in such a good blackmailing position in her whole brief existence.

"Make me an offer," she said, pulling free of his grip and crossing her arms.

Langston racked his brain, while his shell bent over, puzzling over how to tie his sneakers.

Just then Langston spotted a mob of Banneker basketball cheerleaders approaching from the gym.

"Yeeeeeee! *There* he is!" a cute blonde squealed, pointing at Langston. "The hero hottie of Banneker High!"

"Huh?"

The girls screamed in ecstasy and barreled straight for Langston.

Kowabunga! Langston grabbed Alpha with one hand and yanked his shell up with the other, then dragged them down the hall at a run before the cheerleaders could see his shell's face. *God—where to hide, where to hide?*

Hallelujah! The cafeteria's unlocked! Langston pushed Alpha and his shell inside, jumped in after them, and let the double doors swing shut behind them. Gasping to catch his breath, Langston took a quick peek out into the hall through the crack between the doors. The screaming mob of girls dashed right by. Thank God— he'd lost them!

Alpha stood there scowling, tapping her foot.

"*Well,* Mr. Hottie?" she reminded him. "What's your offer?"

"I've got it! Sometime when your mom's not home, I'll baby-sit. And then I'll take you back in the laser machine sixty-six million years. And show you some real, live dinosaurs!"

Of course, Langston knew that after Thursday there wouldn't be another time-travel window for another 888 years—but he figured he'd come up with *something*.

"Even *Stegosaurus*?" Alpha asked.

"Any kind—whatever you want."

"My encyclopedia says *Stegosaurus* was egg-stinked by then."

"Well, that's not my fault. What do you expect me to do about it?" Langston said, losing patience with her.

Alpha made a pouty face, turned, and ran out the doors.

Langston chased desperately after the little girl.

"Alpha! Wait! Okay, okay, I'm sorry!" he said, catching up with her and pulling her back into the cafeteria. "Then, we'll go back as far as it takes to see the dinosaur you want."

"Well . . . all right. But if there's no *Stegosaurus*, I'm gonna tell Mom!"

CHAPTER XXXIV

Oxford, England—January 18, 1278

Dr. Bacon and Niles were packing the friar's three-volume encyclopedia into a straw-filled crate.

"Done at last!" Bacon said. "Niles, this is the most glorious day of my life! Once the pope reads my work, he'll disseminate this knowledge throughout the world. No child need ever again grow up as woefully ignorant as you are."

Niles smiled weakly. Bacon handed him a magnifying glass.

"That is for you," the old man said, "for helping me transcribe my encyclopedia."

Niles examined the strange object, having no idea what it was used for. "Thanks, Father. No one ever give me nothing before. I'm sure I . . . always been needing one of these."

"It's a magnifying lens. It makes things grow bigger."

Bacon demonstrated the magnifying glass, showing Niles how it enlarged the words printed on a page.

"Ayy!" Niles said. "Can it grow a ha'penny into a shilling?"

Bacon and Niles stood on the dock by the Thames River as a sailor loaded their precious crate onto the river barge *Magnifico*. The box was addressed POPE CLEMENT IV, THE LATERAN PALACE, ROME.

"Don't worry, doctor," the sailor said. "We'll get it there all right."

"Godspeed!" Bacon shouted, waving, as the barge sailed away on its ten-day journey.

Meanwhile, in Rome, the pope was resting. There was a knock on his chamber door.

"Avanti!" the pope called out.

One of his aides entered the room.

"Sorry to disturb you, Your Holiness, but something just arrived for you that I thought you might wish to see immediately." He handed the pope a beautiful green glass bottle.

"Ah! French wine!"

"There's a note," the aide said, handing it to him.

The pope read the elegantly inscribed parchment page aloud: "'In honor of the anniversary of your

investiture.' What a thoughtful gesture! Hmmm . . ."
He turned the note over. "That's odd—no signature.
Just, 'A Friend.' I wonder who it could be?"

"The messenger did not say who sent it," the aide said.

"Strange . . . well, it was certainly very thoughtful of
whoever it was, nonetheless. I am sure the good man
who sent this wine will make himself known to me in
due course. *Grazie*, Marcello."

The man knelt, bowing his head, then exited the
chamber.

The pope opened the bottle and sniffed at the wine.
He often had a sip or two of wine before his afternoon
nap to smooth his way to sleep, but this one promised
to be something special. Anticipating great pleasure, he
poured himself a glass and took a sip.

· · · · ·

Jerome of Ascoli stood in the shadows of an alley,
counting coins into the hand of a man who looked like
he had spent his whole life up to no good.

"That's your share," Jerome said. "The rest is for
your friend in Rome who delivered my little . . . gift."

"I'll see that my friend gets it, Brother."

"Yes. I'm sure you will," Jerome said, smiling.

· · · · ·

Back in L.A., Langston sent Alpha off to find her mother, then yanked his shell into the cafeteria's storage closet.

"I hope this thing will work indoors," Langston said, taking the laser remote control device out of his pocket.

He turned to his shell.

"Listen. I gotta go. Be good. But not *too* good. Uh . . . don't do anything I wouldn't do."

Langston pushed the shell out of the closet.

Then, with the DVD player attached firmly to his belt, Langston pressed the button that would bounce him back to Roger Bacon's England.

Langston found Dr. Bacon in the most extraordinary condition. He was sitting alone at the table working on some sort of mechanical device, which he concealed under his habit the moment Langston materialized. Bacon's face was flushed, his speech sounded like his mouth was full of marbles, and his movements were clumsy.

"Here's to Guy Foulques," the doctor said, raising a tankard of ale unsteadily toward Langston. "Better known to most as Clement the Fourth. A great enemy of ignorance. And a great friend to Roger Bacon." He took another swig of ale, nearly slipping off his chair in the process.

Could it be? The great Roger Bacon was plastered!

Bacon raised the tankard in a toast.

"Rest in peace, old man," he said, taking another gulp of ale.

"Dr. Bacon! What's wrong?"

"Pope Clement is no more."

"Dead?"

"Poisoned. Earlier this afternoon in Rome—by a bottle of wine."

"Murdered? How? Wait! How'd you get the news so fast?"

"A message from the pope's valet. By carrier falcon!"

"Who killed the pope?" Langston asked.

"I have my suspicions. But, alas—I have no proof."

"That Jerome guy?"

Dr. Bacon nodded.

"I'm really sorry. I know what it's like to lose a friend."

"So you have explained. In prodigious detail."

"Where's Niles?"

"I sent him away. I did not want to be . . . a bad influence on the lad."

"A bad influence? On a pickpocket? Look, doc, we have to get you sobered up right away. I need to show you something important, and you can't be stewed when you see it."

Langston glanced around the house. "Have you got any coffee?"

"Coffee?"

"Oh, yeah. You English people drink tea, don't you? Well, I guess that might work."

Langston searched the table and found a glass bottle Bacon had labeled CAMELLIA SINENSIS, GIFT OF MARCO POLO. Langston removed the stopper and sniffed the crushed greenish leaves inside.

"Eureka!" he said, recognizing the sweet, woodsy smell.

Over the next hour Langston boiled up pot after pot of tea for the doctor. He walked him around, hoping he'd soon flush out the effects of the alcohol.

"Sleep, sweet slumber . . . ," Bacon said, starting to nod off.

"No!" Langston said, shaking him. "Don't go to sleep! There isn't much time!" He tried to think of something that might keep Bacon awake. "Look, do you know any songs?"

Bacon sang with great feeling, in a surprisingly pleasant baritone:

> "Alas, my love, you do me wrong,
> To cast me off discourteously.
> For I have loved you well and long,
> Delighting in your company.
> Greensleeves was all my joy,
> Greensleeves was my delight,
> Greensleeves was my heart of gold,
> And who but my Lady Greensleeves.
>
> "Your vows you've broken, like my heart.
> Oh, why did you so enrapture me?

Now I remain in a world apart,
But my heart remains in captivity."

Langston joined in on the second chorus:

"Greensleeves was all my joy,
Greensleeves was my delight,
Greensleeves was my heart of gold,
And who but my Lady Greensleeves."

Dr. Bacon sighed, looking sad and wistful.

"Who was she?" Langston asked gently.

"We met when I was a young man. Before my ordination. In the end she chose another man. So I chose the Franciscans. We both made the right decision."

Bacon cleared his throat. "You have a fine voice, m'lad," he said. "Have you ever considered becoming a castrato and joining the boys' choir?"

"Becoming a what?"

"You know . . . ," Bacon said, then sang in a high falsetto voice, "like this."

"No. I don't think so," Langston said, uneasy. "How are you feeling now?"

"Quite sober. Perchance, too sober."

"I have something to show you," Langston said.

CHAPTER XXXV

Langston hit the Play button on the DVD player. Bacon stared in amazement at images from the twentieth and twenty-first centuries. Of course, he was just as fascinated by the remarkable machine that produced them as by the images he was seeing. But what really caught his attention were the horrifying pictures: soldiers being mowed down by the thousands in the World War II D-day invasion; the famous film of a Vietnamese man putting a gun to the head of a civilian and pulling the trigger during the Vietnam War; President John F. Kennedy's skull being blown off in Abraham Zapruder's film of the 1963 assassination, and Jack Ruby shooting President Kennedy's killer, Lee Harvey Oswald, in the belly on "live" television; grainy films of the massacre of 1.5 million Armenians by the Turks during and after World War I; Joseph Stalin's purges, which slaughtered millions of Russians; the 1930s invasion of Manchuria by the

Japanese, who killed tens of thousands of Chinese people; German Nazis killing millions of Jews in towns and death camps during World War II; the fighting on the streets of Beirut, Lebanon; modern gun battles between the Arabs and the Israelis; Protestants killing Catholics in Northern Ireland; American National Guardsmen shooting students at Kent State University during the war protests of the 1960s and 1970s; urban gang violence; the war in Iraq; and on and on.

Langston narrated the whole thing so Dr. Bacon would know exactly what he was seeing. And he told him of the wars that happened before movie cameras could record them, including the American Civil War, which had left more than five hundred thousand men dead.

When it was all over, Langston hit the Stop button and turned to Bacon.

The doctor sighed slowly, staring straight ahead.

"All right," he said quietly.

Langston could hardly believe what he'd heard. "You'll do it? You'll burn your formula for gunpowder?"

Dr. Bacon paused for what seemed to be an eternity. Finally he nodded.

Langston leaned over and crushed Dr. Bacon in a bear hug.

"A little less exuberance," the friar said, peeling Langston off him.

As Langston lifted the DVD player from the table, he heard something fall to the floor behind him. Langston picked up the object. It was a strange, small contraption made of metal that had fallen out of Bacon's habit.

"What is this?" he asked Bacon.

Dr. Bacon suddenly seemed very nervous.

"Nothing. Nothing at all," he said, reaching quickly to snatch it away.

But by now Langston had taken a close look at it, and he glowered at Bacon, furious. "You've already gone and done it, haven't you?"

Bacon looked guilty. "It's . . . it's just a model," he said. "It works, of course, but it's a bit temperamental."

Langston stood silently.

"My initial plan," Bacon continued, with growing enthusiasm, "involved lighting the fuse from the outside. But then any time it rains, you see, the flame would go out. Most inconvenient! That set me to pondering. If some sort of flint serpentine struck sparks into the pan of powder—"

"How could you do this to me? How could you!"

Bacon stood up and slammed the model gun down on the table.

"To *you*? Let me remind you, m'lad, that until you decided to amuse yourself by leaving your own century, I knew nothing of weapons such as this!"

Langston realized the doctor was right. If he hadn't

told Dr. Bacon what guns were, the scientist would never have known anything about them.

Langston picked up the weapon again and examined it.

"Guns aren't supposed to be invented for another twenty-two years! And not by you. This'll screw everything up!"

"Well, it's still rather primitive."

Langston cornered him. "You've got to promise me that you'll destroy it! Do it when you burn your formula for gunpowder."

Bacon took the gun, turning it over in the candlelight and examining it admiringly from all angles.

"It can fire six projectiles. And did you observe the workmanship on the barrel? It must come from my mother's side of the family, this knack for the artistic. I remember one day when I was only a lad of seven—"

"Dr. Bacon!"

Bacon seemed to snap back to reality. "Aye?"

"You'll destroy the gun, too," Langston insisted. "Promise!"

Bacon looked at Langston, seeming to think it over. He crossed the room, pressed the Play button on the DVD player, and viewed a few more moments of its chilling images of violence and death. Then he shut off the machine.

"You have my word," he agreed.

Just then there was a knock at the door. It was a messenger delivering a letter.

Bacon put on his spectacles and read it quickly while the courier waited outside for a reply. As he read, Bacon's expression changed from sorrow to joy.

"A Professor Raffier of the National Academy of Sciences has invited me to give a lecture tomorrow. About my experiments. No restrictions! It's in Paris!"

"Cool!" Langston said.

"Yes, it is, rather—this time of year. I shall take my cloak."

Langston was going to explain American slang but decided it would be more trouble than it was worth.

"The National Academy!" Bacon said, hopping about, as excited as a child. "Don't you see? This means my ideas will become public, Jerome or no Jerome."

He turned back to the courier. "Tell them I accept with gratitude."

Bacon started throwing clothes, papers, and scientific equipment into a trunk. "I'll have to leave immediately. There's a boat that crosses the Channel from London at midnight."

"But—you can't! You said you'd destroy the formula! And the gun!"

"Now, now, m'lad. I shall address that matter the moment I return."

He looked under the table. "Have you seen my boots?"

"No. But—"

"What difference will one day make? Now, remember to feed Ptolemy. He favors kippers. You can buy them from the fishmonger. Remove the bones first."

"But the asteroids are going to move! If I don't get back home within seventy-two hours, I'm gonna be stuck here forever! And that zombie shell of mine is going to be running around L.A. without my soul till hell freezes over!"

"Fie! What kind of babbling, tickle-brained folderol—"

"Never mind."

"Do not concern yourself. I shall return with plenty of time to spare. Before midnight on the morrow."

Bacon closed the trunk, but it was so stuffed the lid wouldn't shut all the way.

"Here, sit on this," he directed.

Langston sat on the trunk while Bacon fastened the locks.

"What if you don't make it back in time?" Langston asked. "Please! Let me burn the formula while you're away."

"No! I created it—and I shall *un*create it when I return."

Bacon dragged his trunk down the streets of Oxford as Langston ran after him. They didn't notice someone observe them briefly from the shadows, then turn and walk in the opposite direction.

"Wait!" Langston called out to Bacon. "Let me go with you!"

Bacon waved down a passing wagon. The driver stopped to let the doctor climb aboard. When Langston caught up with them, the wagon pulled away.

"Wait!" Langston called out again. But the driver wouldn't stop.

"When attempting to hail a wagon," Bacon called back to Langston with a wave, "it helps immeasurably to be a priest!"

Someone was snooping around Dr. Bacon's home. He looked over the doctor's books and experiments—taking care not to leave anything noticeably out of place. Then he picked up the model gun and examined it curiously. It didn't hold his interest for long—he couldn't determine what it was or how it worked. He put it down with a shrug.

Then something else caught the intruder's eye. An open book was on the table. It contained a curious code, but the man couldn't decipher it.

"Aha!" Jerome of Ascoli said to himself after a while. "It's in code. Ow!"

Ptolemy had just used the friar's leg for a scratching post.

"Damn cat!" Jerome said, kicking the animal away.

He returned his attention to the coded formula. *Must be something of great importance,* he thought, *or why bother to disguise it?*

Jerome picked up Bacon's quill, dipped it into ink, and copied the coded words onto a piece of parchment.

"'Live poxes'?" he read the first two words aloud. "Hmmm . . . some sort of pestilence?"

He shuffled the letters around on the page, scratching them out, rearranging them, until . . .

"'Explosive'!"

Jerome banged his fist on the table in triumph. "It's the formula for an explosive!"

Suddenly he heard a sound. Had someone come in?

No—incredibly, the sound was coming from a small, round box with a screen! Jerome's fist had accidentally punched the Play button on the DVD player. He stood transfixed, watching the violent images as they flashed across the small video screen, listening to the sound of explosions and bullets as they wreaked their deadly destruction, tearing into flesh and bone.

"And that's what the explosive can do! Roger, I didn't give you nearly enough credit, my friend. You're a visionary! Another Cassandra the soothsayer!"

Jerome noticed a loose page hanging out of the book. He studied it. The page had a schematic drawing of the model gun. It detailed its moving parts, and notes explained that it could fire six shots.

Jerome picked up the model gun again, recognizing it as the device in the drawing.

He compared the gun with the images on the DVD screen. *Yes—it's the same!* he thought. Jerome's eyes sparkled with delight as the gory images danced in front of them.

"With a weapon like this," he said calmly, "a man could conquer the world."

Jerome's thoughts were interrupted by a sound at the door. He had only barely enough time to hide—before Langston entered the room.

CHAPTER XXXVI

At first Langston didn't notice anything was different at Dr. Bacon's house. But as he passed by the DVD player . . .

That's funny, Langston thought to himself. *The power's on! I'm sure I remembered to turn it off before I left.* . . .

Langston wondered if maybe all his travel through space and time might have scrambled the DVD player's computer chip. Maybe the solar storm had messed it up—or something had been knocked loose when he'd dropped the machine. But still, Langston felt uneasy.

He listened carefully for any suspicious sounds—but heard nothing.

Langston turned the DVD player's power off. Then he sat in Dr. Bacon's chair with Ptolemy on his lap and drifted into a restless sleep.

. . . . .

In L.A. the next morning Langston's shell was sitting in the front row of Mr. Birnbaum's algebra class at Benjamin Banneker High.

"If X is the denominator, you multiply the numerator on the right side by X and the numerator on the left side by the denominator on the left side of the equation," Mr. Birnbaum droned on, and wrote on the blackboard. "No, that's not right . . . I mean, you multiply the numerator on the left side by the denominator on . . ."

Several students groaned. It was always hard for anyone to stay awake in Mr. Birnbaum's class. But Langston's shell did them one better. He got up from his chair, lay down on the teacher's desk, and fell fast asleep—snoring loudly.

Carrying volumes of notes, Dr. Bacon entered a lecture hall in Paris.

How extraordinary! he thought. *No one is here yet.*

Bacon looked at his pocket watch to make sure he was there at the correct time. He was. And he was certain he had come to the right place.

"Hello!" he called out. "I'm Roger Bacon. Is anyone—"

He heard something off to his side. "Professor Raffier?"

But before he could say anything more, a hand was clapped tightly over Dr. Bacon's mouth, and someone grabbed him roughly from behind.

Within seconds Dr. Bacon was bound in ropes. A burlap sack was thrown over his head, and his shouts were muffled into silence.

When the sack was finally removed, Dr. Bacon found himself sitting on a stool behind bars in what looked like a dungeon.

"Release me at once!" he demanded of a burly prison guard who smelled like he hadn't bathed since the reign of King Charlemagne. The man locked Bacon in his cell and pocketed the key.

"There must be some mistake! Where is Professor Raffier? He will tell you who I am!"

"I am so sorry to disappoint you," the Frenchman replied, "but Professor Raffier does not exist. *Tant pis!* The English, are they all as noisy as you, *Père* Bacon?"

"By what law—by whose authority—do you dare detain me? I'm a citizen of the British Crown!"

"And you are also a Catholic friar. Consider yourself a permanent guest, *monsieur,* of our next pope: Jerome."

The man exited, leaving Dr. Bacon entirely alone.

Some hours later a different guard arrived with a surprisingly large plate of food and a cup of cider with a very rare delicacy—a wedge of lemon—in it. He slid the plate and cup under the bars of Bacon's cell.

"You shall eat well here, *monsieur.* After all, this is Paris!"

"How reassuring," Bacon replied with a tone of contempt. "What happened to my large, odiferous friend?"

"He had other business today. You shall see him again."

"How delightful," Bacon replied.

"You have a visitor, *monsieur.*"

"Oh?"

Moments later a dashing young man sporting a neatly trimmed beard, a red cape, and shiny boots was let inside Bacon's cell. The guard locked them in together and left them alone.

"Who are you?" Bacon asked the man. "My executioner?"

"Shhh!" the man replied, a finger to his lips. He looked around to make sure no one was watching, then whispered, "Your savior, I hope, *Padre. Buon giorno,* I am Giacomo Polo, the cousin of Marco Polo."

Bacon crossed himself. "Thank God! But . . . how did you know I was here?"

"The scullery maid who works here. She is a . . . friend of mine. She is also the mistress of that unpleasant fellow who brought you here."

"I see."

"I bribed your guard. He will give me *cinque minuti* with you."

"The Church does not approve of bribery, *signore,*" Dr. Bacon said.

"Please, Father, this is no time for sermons. *Il tempo vola!* Time flies!"

"Can you get me out of here?"

"The problem, she is not so simple. But I can carry a message for you. Do you know anyone who might be able to help you?"

Bacon nodded.

"*Bene.* Good."

Footsteps approached.

"*Presto!* The guard is returning."

Thinking quickly, Bacon searched the floor of his cell and found an iron nail. He gulped down his cider and squeezed the lemon into the empty cup. Bacon dipped the nail into the lemon juice.

"Quick!" he told Giacomo. "Get something to write upon!"

Giacomo handed him a bit of parchment from his pocket.

Bacon scribbled a note on it, using the nail for a pen and the lemon juice as ink. He blew on the note to dry it quickly, then gave it to Giacomo, who folded it and hid it under his cape.

"Get this to the boy Langston at my home on Orchard Lane in Oxford," Bacon whispered urgently. "He'll know what to do with it."

Giacomo nodded.

"You there!" the guard said, entering Bacon's cell.

"What were you writing? Let's see that note!"

"But *signore*, there is no note!" Giacomo said.

The guard suddenly held a knife to his throat. "Then, you won't mind if I search you, eh?" he said with a vicious smile.

"*Per favore*, be my guest!" Giacomo said.

The guard searched Giacomo and found the note. "*Voilà!*" he said in triumph, unfolding the parchment. "Thought you could fool me, *oui*?" But then he looked at the paper—flipping it over, front and back. There was nothing written on it! The guard stared at Giacomo and Bacon, astounded.

"I told you so," Giacomo said, holding out his hand. "May I have it back now? Parchment is *molto costoso—* very expensive, you know."

Still suspicious, the guard reluctantly handed the note back to Giacomo.

· · · · ·

Langston's shell was lying on a couch in the high school psychologist's office, having been sent there by Mr. Birnbaum and the principal. Most of the students found this doctor so annoying that they avoided him as much as possible, so this was the first patient he'd had in ages.

"Now, just relax," the psychologist said. "But not too

much. We don't want you falling asleep again! Har-har-har (snort)!"

The shell shut his eyes. "Yes, Daddy."

"Good!" the psychologist said. "Good transference. I want you to think of me as a member of your own family. Now, I know I'm not of the African-American persuasion. I'm just a stuffy old white doctor. But I can talk the jive, if you know what I mean—har-har-har (snort)."

The psychologist got out a pen and pad, ready to take notes. "I want you to think about home. Just let your mind float free. Free as an eagle on a windy summer day . . . now, tell me the first thing that comes to your mind."

"There are aliens living among us, and they're called teenagers!" the shell recited in Dr. Phil's Oklahoma accent. "Do you really know your kids? Do they know you? On today's show we'll find out what really makes these aliens tick. . . ."

The psychologist took it all down on his notepad, writing furiously. He was already certain that this unusual case study of a patient with multiple personality disorder and manic-depressive tendencies would be a good one to submit to the *Journal of Psychology*.

CHAPTER XXXVII

The arrowlike hands of the primitive clock on the wall of Dr. Bacon's home crept toward midnight. Langston had been waiting anxiously all day for the doctor's return, with little more to keep him occupied than puzzling over Bacon's indecipherable scientific notes and ancient books or throwing a yarn ball for the cat.

"Cuckoo! Cuckoo! . . ."

Finally a wretched-looking wooden bird emerged repeatedly from a little window in the clock, below the scripted words TEMPUS FUGIT, Latin for "Time flies."

"Ten . . . eleven . . . twelve!" Langston counted as the bird finished its croaking. "Midnight. Come on, Dr. Bacon, you promised! Where are you?"

Langston went to the door and looked out for the hundredth time that day. But Dr. Bacon was nowhere to be seen.

A while later, as Langston was going back inside the

house, he heard the thundering sound of hoofbeats. A bearded man in a red cape charged up on a magnificent black stallion that was foaming at the mouth in exhaustion.

"Whoa!" the man said, pulling up sharply on the reins. "*Buona sera!* You are Langston?"

Langston nodded.

The man reached inside his cape, removed a note, and thrust it at Langston.

"From Dr. Bacon. He said you would know what to do."

"Who are you?" Langston asked.

Giacomo Polo looked around anxiously. "A friend. *Mi scusi*, I must go. The spies, they are everywhere! Do not worry. The doctor—*sta bene!*"

And with that Giacomo galloped away.

Langston ran inside the house. Hands shaking, he unfolded the note and saw that it was blank. Frantic, Langston dashed back out into the street.

"Wait!" he shouted to the rapidly retreating form of Giacomo Polo. "Come back! You've given me the wrong . . ."

But it was too late. Giacomo was already out of earshot.

Dejected, Langston shuffled back inside. He crumpled up the note and threw it on a burning log in the fireplace.

But then suddenly it occurred to him: The man couldn't have made a mistake about something so important, could he? *There must be something on that paper!*

Langston grabbed one of the andirons and knocked the burning paper out of the fireplace. He stomped on it to put out the flames.

Fortunately, most of the note was still intact. And strangely, there were now a few brown letters on the parchment that Langston was sure weren't there before. They formed a word! *BEWARE.*

Langston sat down with the parchment. Ptolemy hopped onto his lap, and he petted the cat, thinking. *That note's got to be longer than just one word!*

"What would Mrs. Centauri say?" Langston asked aloud. "'Think like a detective. Or a spy . . .'"

The cat purred and nuzzled his arm, trying to get his attention.

"A spy . . . how do spies write notes, Ptolemy?"

The cat hopped off his lap and kept meowing and scratching at the closet door, but Langston ignored him.

Langston tried to remember all the spy books and movies he'd seen.

"I've got it!" Langston said, standing up suddenly. "Disappearing ink!"

Langston had read a series of children's adventure novels when he was younger, in which spy kids were always writing secret notes in disappearing ink. And what made the hidden letters reappear on the page?

Heat! That's why the fire had made a word reappear on the "blank" note from Dr. Bacon!

Langston dashed over to a candle and held Bacon's parchment a few inches above the flame. Sure enough, more brown letters began to emerge on the surface.

> *Langston:*
> *In Pigale Prison, Paris. Beware of Bro. Jerome.*
> *Destroy formula and gun immediately. Send help.*
> *—Bacon*

My God! Langston thought. *They tricked him! Dr. Bacon's been kidnapped!*

Langston ran to the table where the gun and book containing the formula for gunpowder were kept.

"Oh, no! They're gone! And I gotta be back in L.A. in forty-eight hours!"

Suddenly the closet door burst open, and a man in a friar's habit came flying out of it like a big brown bat, carrying the book and the gun. He shoved Langston out of the way as he barreled toward the door—and out onto the dark street.

As Langston chased after him, the man leaped onto a horse standing outside a smithy's shop and rode away, habit sailing behind him.

"Stop!" Langston shouted, for all the good it would do. He had no horse, so he could not follow.

So, that's Brother Jerome, Langston thought ruefully.

Niles was asleep in a horse trough. A horse was licking his bare toes, and he smiled in his sleep.

A hand shook Niles rudely awake.

"What the . . . ?" Niles squinted and focused his eyes on Langston. "Blimey! You sure know 'ow to ruin a good dream, mate!"

"Get up!" Langston said. "Quick! Dr. Bacon is in jail!"

"Why, the old fox! I didn't know 'e 'ad it in 'im!"

"No—he's been kidnapped! By Brother Jerome's men! He's in Pigale Prison in Paris!"

Niles stood up and put his cap on his head. "Pigale? I been in 'em all an' that's one o' the worst! Food ain't bad, though. . . ."

"Niles, I want you to go there and try to get him out. I'll go after Jerome. He's stolen something important of the doctor's!"

"Didn't know the Father owned anythin' worth stealin', or I mighta tried it meself."

"No time to explain!" Langston said, breathless. "I don't know the roads around here. I'll need some help. I met a girl on the street a few days ago. Do you think you can find her?"

"What's she look like?"

"Skinny. Beautiful. About our age."

"Well, that ain't very 'elpful now, is it?"

"And she's the same color I am."

"Well, crikey, why didn't you say so in the first place!" Langston started running toward the center of town. "Bring her to the doctor's house! I'll meet you there. Hurry!"

"Clock tower . . . clock tower . . . ," Langston muttered, searching the area. Suddenly he heard chimes, then looked up and barely made out in the moonlight a clock at the top of a tall building, with two miniature mechanical twin boys striking bells with hammers to mark the quarter hour. "Ah! There it is!"

He knocked on the door of the house next to the tower. He had to knock a few times before he heard somebody coming down the stairs.

"*Oy,* my back! What kind of *meshuge* . . . ," a voice muttered as it neared the door, "in the middle of the night! Go away!"

"It's me, Mr. Rosenbloom!" Langston cried through the door. "The . . . the boy you took to Oxford! Please—open up!"

Mr. Rosenbloom opened the door. "So? You couldn't maybe have picked the daytime for this little visit?"

"I'm sorry to wake you, Mr. Rosenbloom, but I really need your help. Can I borrow your milk wagon for the day?"

"You got a sudden *yen* for milk? Come in—we'll

nosh, we'll *schmooze.* You can drink all the milk you want!"

"No! I mean, thanks, but it's your wagon I need. Please—trust me! There's no time to explain."

"Give you my wagon?" the old man said, raising his hand. "I'll give you a *patsh* on the *tokhes,* that's what I'll give you!"

"But you promised you'd help me! It's for Dr. Bacon, and—"

"Dr. Bacon? The teacher Dr. Bacon?"

"Yes! That's him."

"He's on my rounds! Two jugs of milk every morning. And one cream for that kitty of his. Such a nice *goy!*"

"Then, you'll help me? It's a matter of life and death!"

"So serious? Well, in that case . . . the wagon is in the barn behind the house. But take good care of it!"

"Thank you! I promise—you'll never regret this! By the way . . . uh . . . could you please feed Dr. Bacon's cat while I'm away?"

CHAPTER XXXVIII

Langston tried to stop the wagon as he neared Dr. Bacon's home, but he didn't know the command to halt the horses, and they kept on going.

"Whoa! Uh . . . cease! Tallyho! Whatever . . ."

He quickly discovered that words didn't work. But fortunately a tug on the reins was all it took to stop them.

Niles came running up with the African girl. Langston's brain seemed to turn to oatmeal the moment he saw her again.

"Uh . . . it's you. You're here!" he said, wishing he could think of something brilliant to say.

"I promised I would be, if you ever needed me."

Niles helped her up into the wagon, onto the seat beside Langston.

"I explained it all to 'er," Niles said. "Don't worry, mate. I'll get the old doc out!"

"Thanks. Good luck!" Langston called as Niles

dashed quickly away. Langston turned to the girl.

"Did he tell you that this trip could be dangerous? I don't want you to get hurt. You don't have to do this, you know. I can still take you back if you want. And I won't think any less of you. Honest."

"I want to help you," the girl said, determination in her voice.

"Good. That man Jerome we're chasing—he's got a few hours' head start on us."

"Which direction?"

"I wish I knew. Wait—I *do* know! Dr. Bacon told me that Jerome is going to be elected pope. I think they hold those meetings at the college of cardinals in Edinburgh. Jerome's bound to be there. Which way is Scotland?"

She pointed north. "Take that road. It's a shortcut!"

Langston and the girl had traveled a long distance, but still they had seen no sign of Jerome.

"We'll never find him," Langston despaired as their wagon trundled along the bumpy road.

"You must not give up. What does this Jerome have that belongs to your friend?"

"It's a——some kind of weapon. If it gets into the wrong hands, it'll hurt a lot of people."

"Then, we shall find him," the girl said, "and stop him!"

Langston was impressed by her gumption but didn't have the nerve to say so.

"By the way, I forgot to ask you," he said, embarrassed. "I'm Langston. What's your name?"

"Ngala."

"That's beautiful. Is it African?"

"Yes, of course. I was born a slave in North Africa. When I was around eight, they took me from my mother and sold me to a man in the Holy Land."

"That's awful!"

"I haven't seen her in seven years. I fear if I saw her now, I might not know her face."

Langston could see the glint of tears in Ngala's eyes. He wished he knew what to say to comfort her.

"Three years ago," Ngala continued, "my master sold me to one of the Christians who came to the Holy Land with King Edward on a Crusade. It was that man who brought me to England . . . it is good to be free."

"Yes," Langston said, "it is."

"You escaped from your master also?"

"My country hasn't got any slaves. Not anymore."

"It must be a wonderful place. Where is your home?" Ngala asked.

Langston sighed. "A million lifetimes away. Uh . . . I mean, it seems that way. I've only got till tomorrow night before I gotta go back."

"Oh." Ngala sounded disappointed.

"Uh . . . you hungry?" Langston asked, breaking the

awkward silence that fell between them. "I mean, we haven't had anything to eat all day."

She nodded.

"It's nearly sundown. We better stop soon for a quick rest anyway, since we've got to drive through the whole night. I wouldn't want to fall asleep at the wheel. Uh . . . I mean, at the reins."

After a few more minutes they rode up to a farm.

"This looks like as good a place as any," Langston said. "We can rest here, and there's plenty of milk in the back of the wagon. I'm sure Mr. Rosenbloom won't mind if we have some."

Langston brought the horses to a stop and lifted one of the milk jugs off the back of the wagon. He sniffed at it.

"Ugh," he said. "Spoiled! Guess it's unpasteurized."

"What?"

"Nothing. Look, we'll have to find something else to eat. If you drink this stuff, it'll make you sick."

They opened the door to the barn.

"Milk!" the girl said cheerfully, pointing to a cow.

"If we can figure out how to get it out of Bossie here . . . ," Langston said.

"Don't you know how?"

"Well . . . I never really had to. The cows put their milk in little boxes where I come from."

Ngala looked puzzled. "You are strange sometimes," she said.

"Oh," Langston said, hurt.

"But a nice kind of strange."

"Oh," he said, "that's good."

They walked into the barn.

"Don't worry," Langston said. "Just wait here. I'll find you something to eat. There's got to be food around here somewhere. . . ."

Ngala picked up a wooden bucket, crouched down by the cow, reached underneath—and in seconds Langston heard a steady *swish! swish! swish!* as the cow's milk squirted into the bucket.

"Where'd you learn to do that?" Langston asked, impressed.

Ngala just smiled at him.

Then they both laughed.

CHAPTER XXXIX

While Langston and Ngala were on their way to Scotland, Niles was desperately trying to get to Paris to rescue Bacon.

"'Elp! Man overboard! Man overboard!" Niles shouted as he swam furiously toward a boat that had just set sail from the English side of the Channel. Of course, he hadn't really fallen off the boat and wasn't really drowning.

A hulking French sailor threw him a rope and pulled him aboard.

"Thanks, mate," Niles said, shivering like a wet weasel. "Don't know what I woulda done wivout you. This ship 'eaded for Paris?"

"*Oui, garçon.* By way of Calais."

The sailor started to walk away, then seemed to realize something.

"*Un moment . . . ,*" he said, suspicious. "I thought you said you fell *off* this boat?"

"Uh . . . that's right," Niles replied nervously.

"Then, why don't you know where we're going?"

When the ship docked at Calais, the sailor tossed Niles onto the dock like a sack of potatoes and brushed his hands together.

"*Bon* riddance!" the sailor growled.

"Well, I'll be damned if I'll give you my patronage again!" Niles shouted back at the sailor, and scrambled to his feet. "Send the bill to Windsor Castle!" He glanced around. "'Ello, France! Your favorite boy is back!"

· · · · ·

Langston and Ngala had drunk all the milk their stomachs would hold, taking turns from the bucket. They leaned against a hay bale to rest.

"Tell me more about your home," Ngala said.

"I live in a city across the sea. It's okay, I guess. But people get killed there a lot."

"Like here."

"Yes," Langston replied.

"Your family, do you miss them?"

"Yes. Sometimes. But we don't always get along."

Ngala sighed. "I wish I had a family to not get along with."

Langston smiled. "I wish you did too."

He caught her staring at him—and thought he'd give anything to know what she was thinking.

"Well," he said, feeling awkward, "maybe we should try to catch some sleep. You rest over here. I'll . . . uh . . . sit over there and wake you in a little while." He pointed to a bale of hay on the opposite side of the barn. "Then I'll sleep for a bit, and you can wake me."

Ngala shivered.

"You're cold!" Langston said. He took off his Anaheim Angels jacket and gently covered her shoulders with it. Just being that near to her, Langston suddenly realized he'd never felt so good in his life. He noticed she didn't seem to mind when it took him practically forever to adjust the jacket on her shoulders.

Then something fell out of the jacket pocket. It was a note. Langston picked it up and read it aloud.

"Hold fast to dreams
For if dreams die
Life is a broken-winged bird
That cannot fly."

"You write very nice ballads," Ngala said.

"No—I didn't write it. It's by a . . . bard I was named after, Langston Hughes. The note—it's in my father's handwriting. He must have slipped it into my pocket the last night I was in—I mean, the last night I was home."

"It is a good ballad," Ngala said.

"I can't believe it! It's not like my dad at all to give me something like this."

"Your father must be a very good man."

This made Langston think.

Then she added shyly: "Like his son."

Ngala's hand touched Langston's. Just a slight brush of the hand, like a butterfly's wing. Almost as if he'd imagined it. Only, he hadn't imagined it.

They looked at each other like two halves of the same soul. Then Langston leaned forward and kissed Ngala—as if he'd been imagining this moment for centuries.

· · · · ·

After hitching rides all the way to Paris, Niles reached Pigale Prison by sunrise on Thursday morning. He sneaked past a sleeping guard and ran from cell to cell, peering into each one. Finally . . .

"Pssst! Guv'nor! Father Bacon!" Niles hissed.

Bacon woke up, squinting in the early-morning sunlight that streamed through the window bars.

"What? Niles! Where's Langston? Is he all right?"

"Shhh! Yes. I'm gonna spring you!"

"How?"

"Damned if I know," Niles said, shrugging.

"Watch your language."

Bacon paced his cell, trying desperately to come up with a plan. The guard was snoring loudly but could awaken at any moment.

Bacon looked at the window, shading his eyes from the glare.

"Niles!" Bacon said suddenly. "Do you have that magnifying lens I gave you?"

"I thinks so. Why?"

Bacon removed a small glass vial of powder from his pocket. Then he pulled a short strand of thread from the fabric of his habit and passed the vial and string to Niles.

"Put some of this powder in the cell lock. And for God's sake, not too much. Then attach this string to it."

"What? What possibilutely good is that gonna—"

"Don't blather, Niles!" Bacon demanded. "Just do what I say!"

· · · · ·

As the sun rose on the road to Scotland, Langston spotted a rider galloping a few hundred yards ahead of them. Even from the back Langston could see who it was.

"It's Jerome!" Langston said to Ngala. "Hold on tight!" He gave a quick snap of the reins, urging the horses to go faster.

"But what can we do with this Jerome when we catch

up with him?" Ngala asked. "He will not give us what he has stolen. He has nothing to fear from a boy and a girl."

Ngala was right. Langston looked at his watch, which he'd set to medieval English time. *Jeez! Six o'clock in the morning already—and I gotta be back in Oxford by midnight tonight, or I'll never be able to get back to L.A.!*

Just then they passed by an open field on a hill where a thousand English knights in chain mail were assembled on horseback. They had red crosses on their tunics, carried longbows, and were clearly ready for battle.

Opposite them on the field was a somewhat smaller group of men in leather tunics with iron plates sewn onto them. They had smaller horses than their enemies and carried long pikes or spears instead of bows.

"Wow! It's like that old movie *Braveheart!*" Langston said to Ngala, though she didn't know what he was talking about. "Those guys must be the English knights and the Scots!"

The opposing armies let out bloodcurdling yells, then charged toward each other.

Meanwhile, Langston could still see Jerome galloping ahead of them, getting farther away by the minute. They were going to lose him!

Suddenly Langston stopped the wagon, stood up, pointed to the fleeing Jerome, and during a momentary lull in the din of battle yelled toward the English soldiers:

"Knights of the British realm! After that man! He's stolen the Holy Grail!"

"The Grail! The Grail!" the English knights shouted, spreading the word.

Almost immediately a swarm of men changed direction like a crowd doing the wave at a football game.

Jerome glanced behind him and was stunned to see an entire army in full battle gear coming after him.

Of course, Langston knew Jerome didn't really have the Holy Grail. The Grail was Jesus' cup at the Last Supper, which Langston had read about in books on King Arthur and the knights of the Round Table. The knights were always questing after it. Langston never understood why anybody would want the Grail, when the last guy who'd drunk out of it had gotten crucified, but that didn't seem to stop anybody.

Langston and Ngala sped along in their wagon as a thousand bloodthirsty British knights thundered after Jerome, brandishing their swords and longbows.

The Scots stood on the hill, watching the English army retreat and wondering what the hell had happened.

The Scottish commanders shrugged, then raised their spears in the air.

"Victory!" they shouted.

CHAPTER XL

"Steady hand, boy, steady," Dr. Bacon whispered to Niles through the bars of his jail cell.

Niles held the magnifying glass motionless in the correct position. He was carefully focusing a ray of sunlight on their makeshift thread fuse. The thread hung from the cell door's keyhole—which was packed with gunpowder.

"Eureka!" Bacon said in triumph as the fuse finally caught fire and began to sizzle.

Bacon's shout woke the sleeping guard, who barreled toward Niles.

As the fuse burned down to its last quarter inch, Bacon crouched at the back of the cell, getting ready— head down, hands over his ears.

"Run, boy—run!" he shouted to Niles, who took off, forcing his way past the guard, barreling over kitchen help, other guards—anyone who got in his way. Finally another guard caught Niles by the arm. He was trapped!

KABOOM!

The jail cell door blew off its hinges, taking half the ceiling down with it. The guard loosened his grip on Niles just long enough for the boy to wriggle away.

The force of the explosion knocked Dr. Bacon to the floor of his cell.

Fortunately he was only knocked unconscious—and awoke after a few seconds. He shook his head, trying to get the infernal ringing out of his ears. He rose slowly to his knees, then onto his feet. With all the chaos the explosion had caused, Bacon was able to slip out of the prison unnoticed and met Niles outside under a tree, just as they'd planned.

"I said use only a *pinch* of gunpowder, you beetle-headed baggage!" Bacon complained, rubbing his sore head.

"Uh . . . sorry."

"Still," Bacon conceded with a sigh, "you did secure my freedom. You have my gratitude for that."

"Anytime, mate. Er . . . I mean, Father," Niles replied, basking in the doctor's praise.

"What happened to Langston?" Bacon asked.

"'E said Brother Jerome stole somethin' from you— so 'e's gone after 'im."

"The formula!" Bacon exclaimed, his eyes narrowing. "When I think what that craven, rump-fed rapscallion Jerome could do with it . . . quick, m'lad!" He grabbed Niles by the arm. "We must get back to Oxford! And let us pray that Langston is there by the time we arrive!"

. . . . .

Zzzip! Ka-ping!

"Get down!" Langston shouted to Ngala. "Jerome's firing the gun!"

"The what?"

Langston pushed Ngala's head down just as a bullet struck a knight's sword.

"I'll explain later. Just stay down!"

Jerome didn't know how to aim the gun, so it went off wildly.

A procession of monks was crossing the road, walking in rhythm with the sound of church bells ringing in a steeple.

Zzzip! Ka-pong! Jerome's next bullet sailed into the steeple and ricocheted off a bell, souring its notes. The monks lost their rhythm and dominoed into one another, falling in a heap.

That's two. Dr. Bacon had told Langston the gun could fire six shots—Jerome had only four bullets left.

Langston and Ngala's wagon rattled past a public execution.

"By order of His Majesty, King Edward, for the theft of a loaf of bread!" the MC reading the death warrant intoned. "Let the execution proceed!"

A pathetic, trembling prisoner put his head on the chopping block, and just as the black-masked executioner lowered his ax toward the man's neck . . .

Zzzip! Ka-ping!

Three.

The stray bullet from Jerome's gun knocked the ax blade off. Nobody could figure out what had happened, and in the confusion that followed, the condemned prisoner escaped.

Zzzip! Ka-pow!

Four.

There was a crunching noise as the wagon suddenly skidded into a muddy ditch and lurched to a stop.

"Are you all right?" Langston asked Ngala, holding her.

"Yes, what happened?"

Langston hopped out of the wagon. "It's the tire! I mean . . . the wheel! It's broken!"

"Can you fix it?"

"Uh . . . no. I don't know how."

"But you must! Jerome will get away!"

"I can't! I don't know how to do everything, you know!"

Langston was disgusted with himself, especially for snapping at Ngala. He could see she looked hurt.

"I'm sorry," he said.

But what else could he say? He slumped on the ground.

Ngala got out of the wagon and put an arm around Langston's shoulders.

"Please. Try," she said.

She kissed him.

And in that kiss Langston found his courage.

Langston picked up a log by the roadside and used it to prop up the wagon. He went around to the back to look among the milk jugs for some kind of tool that might help him.

"Well, what do you know!" he said. "There's a spare!"

Langston brought the spare wheel and a tool around to the front, and within a few minutes he'd replaced the old one. And they were soon back on the road.

"You are my knight in shining armor!" Ngala said.

Within half an hour, the knights had Jerome and his horse cornered, their backs toward a windmill. Its blades rotated slowly in the breeze. The knights surrounded Jerome, rattling their swords, longbows poised to fire at him.

"Get the Grail!" an English commander said to one of the knights, who moved in to grab Jerome.

At precisely that moment Langston and Ngala rode up in their wagon.

Jerome slowly backed his horse up against the windmill, raised his gun, and aimed it straight at Ngala.

"Call off the knights!" he warned Langston. "Or I'll shoot the girl!"

Langston didn't dare move. Ngala didn't know what guns were, but she knew she had something to fear. They were trapped.

"Please!" Langston said to the English commander. "Don't touch him! He'll kill my friend!"

"Fie! He has no weapon!" the commander said. "Out of our way!"

Jerome cocked the gun trigger. Langston threw Ngala to the ground, covering her with his own body just as the shot rang out.

Zzzip! Ka-ping!

The shot whizzed just over their heads, bouncing off a plow. The knights' horses reared at the sharp sound of the gun going off.

Five. He's got one bullet left!

Suddenly Jerome rose in the air.

"What the . . . ?" he said, his head swiveling around.

A windmill blade had gotten caught in the friar's habit and lifted Jerome straight up off his horse. The blades creaked to a stop, leaving Jerome suspended pre-cariously more than thirty feet above the ground.

"Help me!" Jerome squawked, watching his riderless horse gallop away.

"The wind has stopped! Now we'll get him!" one of the knights shouted.

"Run him through!" cried another.

The other knights growled their approval, drawing their bows.

"No—wait!" Langston called. He shouted to Jerome, "Hang on! I'll try to save you!"

Langston dashed up the stairs of the windmill. Jerome's cloak was hanging by a thread on the blade. He could fall at any moment.

"Hurry!" Jerome was terrified, looking down at the long drop to the ground. "You'll be well rewarded by the Church! I promise!"

"I don't want your money, you scuzz-bucket!"

Langston reached the top of the windmill. He tried to pull Jerome inside through its small window by grabbing on to his hood, but the man was too heavy.

"Give me your hand," Langston said.

Just as Jerome reached for his hand, the fabric of his habit finally tore through.

He screamed, plummeting to the ground.

A few moments later Langston and Ngala stood next to Jerome's lifeless form. On the ground next to him were Dr. Bacon's book and the model gun, both of which Langston picked up.

"The Grail, the Grail, the Grail!" the knights chanted, moving in on their horses for a closer look at the items.

But they saw only the book and the gun in Langston's hands.

"That ain't the Grail!" said a fat knight who was carrying a mace.

A couple of other knights dismounted and searched Jerome's body.

"It's not here!" one of them announced to the group.

Finally the fat knight pointed to Langston.

"Kill him!" he said.

Langston grabbed Ngala's hand and dragged her up into their wagon.

"Eeyahh!" he yelled to the horses, snapping the reins. They took off at a hard gallop back toward Oxford, with a thousand very angry English knights riding after them.

CHAPTER XLI

"Dump the milk jugs off the back!" Langston said to Ngala as they drove madly across a very narrow bridge with the knights in pursuit.

Ngala scrambled into the back of the wagon and sent the jugs rolling out onto the road, blocking the bridge and causing a huge pileup of English knights and horses who couldn't stop in time to avoid them.

Langston took a quick look behind him. Relieved, he saw that they were no longer being followed.

Langston pulled up on the reins in front of Dr. Bacon's house in Oxford. He looked at his watch. Thank God! It was only eleven forty-five. He'd arrived with fifteen minutes to spare.

Ngala turned to him. "I shall return the wagon to its owner for you. I will explain we didn't drink all that milk."

"Thanks, Ngala . . . I . . ."

Langston didn't know what to say. He knew that

there'd be no way on earth he could ever see her again. His stomach hurt—or maybe his heart. He'd come here to try to save one friend, and now he was about to lose another.

"You must go?" Ngala asked.

He nodded.

"You shall remember me in your home across the sea?"

"Forever," he said.

"Then, I shall not see you again?"

"I wish, I really wish I could," Langston said. "I . . . I don't see how."

"Remember what your father told you," she said, hugging him.

"'Hold fast to dreams' . . . I'll remember . . . good-bye."

They kissed—one last dream that Langston wished could go on forever.

Langston handed the book and gun back to Dr. Bacon, who was sitting by the fireplace next to Niles.

"Thank you, Langston," Bacon said. "I know you went to some great difficulty to return these to me."

"It was worth it."

Bacon nodded. He stood slowly, extending the book toward the fire. The bright flames licked at the edges of its calfskin binding.

But then something made him hesitate. Bacon withdrew the book from the fire, turned, and sat back down in his chair.

"I am sorry," he said. "I can't."

"Blimey!"

"What? But . . . but you promised!" Langston added to Niles's protest. "If you don't destroy that book, my friend will die!"

"I know," Bacon said. "And millions of others who were loved just as much will perish as well. And if my destroying this book would bring even one of them back, I would do it in an instant."

Bacon stood abruptly, rapidly yanking books off the shelves. He slammed them down on the table, one on top of the other, in front of Langston.

"Aristotle, Avicenna, al-Ghazali, Confucius! Ancient Greek, Hebrew, Latin, Arabic!"

Bacon knocked the tower of books down with a sweep of his hand.

"Explosives. They've been described in every land, in every language! Langston, do you honestly believe that if I burn my book, the world will never learn of this weapon?"

The doctor opened one very dusty book to a page marked with a bookmark, and pointed. The writing was in a foreign language and showed a drawing of an explosion. Niles stood up to peer at the book's illustrations.

"Crikey, looka 'ere! A whole blinkin' bridge, an' they blown it to nothin' but fairy dust!"

"This is Greek fire!" Dr. Bacon continued. "The ancient Greeks knew of explosives a thousand years before the birth of Christ. At . . . at this very moment there are probably a dozen other scientists in cities around the world who read the ancient languages and have made the same 'discovery' I have!"

"But I thought you invented gunpowder!" Langston said, reaching in his pocket for the encyclopedia article. He unfolded it and handed it to Dr. Bacon. "My friend's encyclopedia says—"

"I never claimed I *invented* it," Bacon said, glancing at the article. "Maybe . . . maybe I wanted you to believe I had. And for the world to believe. 'Roger Bacon's discovery frees the serfs in England.' That would be a fine legacy, would it not? There is no such thing as original research in science. Discovery doesn't spring from the mind of one man, but from the mind of mankind."

Langston didn't know whether he was angrier at Dr. Bacon or at himself, for having trusted him.

"You lied to me!" Langston cried.

"You gotta admit, doc," Niles interjected, "the bloke's got a point."

Bacon reached to put a hand on Langston's shoulder, but Langston twisted away from him.

"I don't care what you say!" Langston protested. "Maybe there are a hundred other guys who will think up gunpowder. Maybe there aren't. But I know of only one guy who got it right. And I'm not leaving here till you burn that book!"

Dr. Bacon dipped a quill pen in a bottle of ink, preparing to write on a piece of parchment.

"What are you doing?" Langston asked.

"Ordering a set of false teeth for you."

"What? Why?"

"Because," Bacon replied, "if you intend to stay here until I burn that book, you're still going to be waiting here when you are a very, very old man."

Niles stifled a laugh.

But Langston just scowled. He looked at his watch. Only eight minutes left!

Suddenly Langston grabbed the gun from the table. He wasn't thinking about anything except Neely—and what he had to do.

With a slow, deliberate motion Langston raised his hand until the gun was pointed right at Bacon's heart.

"Langston!" Niles shouted, moving between them. He didn't know what guns were, but sensed Dr. Bacon was in some sort of terrible danger.

Bacon motioned commandingly for Niles to step out of the way. Reluctantly Niles stepped back.

Bacon slowly extended his hand toward Langston.

"Now, I will thank you to surrender that weapon to me."

"Give me the book!" Langston demanded.

Bacon shook his head and took a step toward

Langston, eyes fixed firmly on the boy's. He took another step, reaching for the gun, which was still just beyond his grasp.

"Keep—keep away from me!" Langston warned, moving his finger toward the gun's trigger.

"Don't!" Niles pleaded.

Langston's hand trembled. He couldn't believe what he was doing, what he was about to do! But he couldn't make himself stop.

Bacon moved slowly toward him, eyes fixed intently on Langston's and burning, not with hatred—and this was the thing that Langston couldn't understand—but with compassion.

"'For what does it profit a man,'" Bacon said to him softly, "'if he shall gain the whole world and lose his own soul?'"

Those words! Words from the Bible, which Langston's mother had read to him so many times.

Suddenly Langston was overcome with shame. He sank to his knees, bowing his head. He had failed everyone—even himself. *I'm sorry, Neely,* he thought. *I tried.*

Bacon put a hand on Langston's shoulder, then knelt and gently took the gun away from him.

Niles exhaled with relief, then slumped down at the table. With unsteady hands he poured himself a drink from a jug, spilling water.

Dr. Bacon went back to his chair by the fire.

Slowly Langston looked up at him.

"You . . . you were so calm," Langston said, his voice shaky with emotion. "Weren't you scared I'd . . . I'd . . ."

"No. I knew you wouldn't."

"How?"

"For one thing, you're a good lad. And for another," he said with the hint of a smile, holding up a piece of paper, "if my first hypothesis proved to be incorrect, your encyclopedia says I don't expire until the year 1292."

"What about the formula? Weren't you worried I'd take it back home with me?"

Bacon shook his head and pointed to his temple.

"It's all in here," he said.

"Oh," Langston said, feeling like a fool. He got up and sat down at the table with Niles.

Bacon lit a candle.

"Langston, listen to me," he said. "Try to understand. I'm an old man. I've spent over half my lifetime trying to conduct and record my experiments despite interference from people who feared what I and the world might learn from them—a world that prefers to live in the darkness of ignorance."

He affixed the lighted candle to a plate, then brought it to the table, sitting down between the boys.

"All those fearful souls have the best of intentions," he continued, "to save mankind from some terrible evil that they believe that progress might bring. And perhaps they are right. But there is an evil far greater than anything the mind of a scientist can create."

He held the candle up before his face and quickly placed a glass jar over it. The candle snuffed out, plunging most of the room into darkness.

"Suppression of free thought."

Bacon stood and walked over to the fireplace. His face, illuminated by the flames, glowed eerily from the darkness like a planet in space.

"If I allowed anyone to persuade me to destroy even one page of my research, I'd be betraying every scholar who has been imprisoned for his beliefs, every man whose book was set ablaze in the public square. And every so-called witch who was burned at the stake."

Bacon crossed back to the table and put his hand on Langston's.

"But the same freedom God gave me to speak out for what I believe, he gave to you. If you don't like where science has led your world, say so. Shout it from the parapets! I've used my voice. Now use yours."

Langston was deeply moved by Bacon's words. But was he persuaded? He didn't really know.

Langston looked at his watch: 11:58.

"I better go." He turned to Niles. "Listen, I—"

"Save your breath, mate," Niles said with an affectionate grin. "The Father expl'ined the whole thing to me on the way from Paris. 'Ope you make it back 'ome all right. Things won't be the same 'round 'ere wivout you."

"Thanks. Take care, okay?" Langston said, thinking how much he'd miss him and how much Niles reminded him of . . . somebody else.

They shook hands. Niles got up from the table, stepped back, and then flipped Langston a coin. Langston caught it in midair and put it in his pocket.

"Don't worry 'bout me," Niles said. "The Father'll keep me on the straight an' narrow. Won't you, Father?"

Bacon put a hand on Niles's shoulder.

"I have decided to adopt Niles as my son," he said.

Langston couldn't be happier for them. Maybe they squabbled like children, but they'd be good for each other.

He looked at his watch again. One minute to go.

Langston stood and gave Ptolemy a final pat good-bye. He took the laser remote control device out of his pocket and punched in the time and place of his destination: home.

"Good-bye, Dr. Bacon," Langston said.

"Good-bye, m'lad. Can you . . . can you ever forgive me?"

Langston looked at him, then smiled. "Oh . . . maybe in about seven hundred years."

The doctor smiled back.

Langston picked up the portable DVD player, then

pressed the Double Voyager Earth Return button on the laser remote control. Just as he was vanishing, he heard Dr. Bacon say: "This much I will do. . . ." He handed Langston the gun.

"It will only briefly delay the inevitable," Bacon said as Langston took the weapon from him, "but destroy it, m'lad. With my blessing."

And then Langston was gone.

CHAPTER XLII

It was one minute after midnight in Los Angeles. Langston's shell and his mother were sitting on the couch eating popcorn—their attention riveted on an old horror movie on TV.

"I walked with a zombie . . . ," a young nurse was narrating in the movie. "It all began in such an ordinary way. . . ."

Two identical right hands, mirror images of each other, opened the door to Langston's apartment a crack, and the hands' owners peeked inside. Then the twin Langstons tiptoed into the living room, behind the couch, and grabbed the shell by the back of the collar, yanking him into the hall. Langston's mother was so involved in the scary movie, she didn't notice he was gone until the next commercial break. And even then she figured he'd probably just gone to bed.

Ring . . . ring . . . ring . . . ring!

An answering machine picked up.

"This is Jerry the Milkman at Strawberry Fields Farms—drink fresh milk and rock your world, baby! The cows and I are out moooovin' and groovin', so—"

Somebody picked up the phone, interrupting the outgoing message. "You've got the real, live, sexy me," Jerry said, purring into the phone. "Hi, honeybaby-gorgeous. You looked really groovy in that miniskirt last night, babe. How about tonight we—"

"Huh? Where were you, man?"

"Langster?"

"We—I mean, *I've* been standing out here in the cold at a pay phone trying to reach you *all night!*"

"Langster! I thought you were my—never mind! I was crashin' at my pad gettin' some z's, kid, what'd ya think I was doin'?"

The milkman reversed the order of his morning and afternoon delivery rounds so he could drive Langston up the mountain to Mrs. Centauri's house. Or, to be more precise, he drove *three* Langstons: the original Langston, his shell, and the other Langston. Jerry and the original Langston put the other two in the back of the truck.

"So, you're uh . . . what do you call it?" Jerry said, thinking. "Triplets!"

"Uh . . . yeah. Kind of . . . ," Langston said, hoping Jerry wouldn't ask too many questions.

"Out of sight! That really blows my mind, man!"

"Yeah, well," Langston said, "I guess it can get pretty complicated for me, too, sometimes."

"Hey—do you ever, I mean, like, go out with the same chick, pretending to be just one of you?"

"Umm . . . well, we don't really date."

The milkman turned his head. "I don't hear anything going on back there. Your brothers don't talk much, do they?"

"Not really," Langston said. "I'm kind of like . . . the spokesman for all of us."

"I dig," the milkman said. "Like John Lennon for the Beatles."

Fortunately, Jerry didn't ask any more questions, and before long he dropped them all off at Mrs. Centauri's. Langston asked him to wait in the truck.

Langston peeked in the door. Luckily, Mrs. Centauri and Alpha were still soundly asleep. Langston went in and used the laser machine to fuse himself back together with his shell and the other Langston. It took only a few minutes, and everything went smoothly.

"Aren't they coming back with us?" the milkman asked when Langston came out to the truck by himself.

"Uh . . . Mrs. Centauri isn't home," he said, loading

his mother's mirror into the back. "They said they wanted to wait for her, but I gotta get to school. Don't worry—she'll drive them down later."

"What you mean going out like that last night, not telling your mama where you're goin'!"

Langston's father had just come home from work and stood nose-to-nose with his son in the living room.

"But I couldn't—you don't understand! You'll never understand!"

"Don't you talk back to me, boy! Always talkin' back! You . . ."

Suddenly his father stopped short. Then he burst out laughing. He laughed louder and louder, doubling over with it.

"What's so funny?" Langston asked angrily.

"*Us!* Goin' at each other like this again. You know," his father said, "I actually like you better this way. Not so 'Yes, Daddy' all the time."

He put a hand on Langston's shoulder. "It's good to have you back, son."

Does he know? Langston looked closely at his father. No, he was certain that his dad didn't suspect a thing.

"It's good to be home," Langston replied, meaning every word of it.

. . . . .

Early on Saturday morning Langston was crouched on the street next to his father's car. Mr. Davis came out of their building shaking his head.

"That Coach called us again. Said some crazy stuff about the NBA draft and you being the next LeBron James. Told him he must have the wrong number."

The day before, so many people at school had congratulated Langston on his great basketball game that he'd guessed what must have happened. But rather than try to explain it to his father, he just loosened the last tire bolt and said, "Okay, Dad."

"Wait a minute!" Mr. Davis said, finally noticing what Langston was working on. "You're changing the tire! Where'd you learn how to do that?"

"From watching you, Dad," Langston said proudly.

His father smiled, turning to go. Then he paused, turned around, and walked back a few steps.

"Langston, I . . . I'm sorry about what happened to Neely. I should have said somethin' before. I—"

"Thanks," Langston said. "It's going to be all right."

CHAPTER XLIII

January 28, 2010

The banner over the stage read, WINTER 2010 BENJAMIN BANNEKER HIGH ACADEMIC ACHIEVEMENT AWARDS. The audience was packed with teachers, parents, and students. Some of the award statuettes—which looked like miniature versions of famous people—had already been presented.

Mrs. Centauri lifted Alpha up to the microphone, since she was too short to reach it.

"Jeez," Mrs. Centauri said, straining to hold her up. "What have we been feeding you? You're getting too big to carry!"

The audience laughed.

"And now," Alpha said, "the award for the best overalls!"

"Overall," Mrs. Centauri whispered in her daughter's ear.

"Oopsie! Overall. The award for the best overall grades in science class by a student in his first se . . . se . . ."

"Semester," Mrs. Centauri prompted.

"Goes to . . . take it away, Mom!"

Mrs. Centauri opened an envelope, then leaned over the microphone. "Langston Davis!"

Langston's family and his squealing basketball groupies led the applause as he trotted up to the stage to accept his award. Alpha handed him a little statuette of Albert Einstein, then tugged on Langston's shirt to get his attention. He bent down, and she whispered in his ear, "Remember, smarty-brain. *Stegosaurus.* Or I tell."

Langston nodded nervously at Alpha.

"Shhh!" he whispered back. "Okay, I promised, didn't I?"

He stepped behind the podium to address the audience.

"Thank you," Langston said into the microphone. "I'd like to thank my science teacher, Mrs. Centauri, and my folks for this award."

He walked away from the podium to polite applause.

"Okay," Mrs. Centauri said to the audience. "And the next award goes to . . ."

But when Langston was halfway off the stage, a strong, insistent voice came to him, echoing across the centuries: *I've used my voice. Now use yours.*

Langston turned back to the podium and asked Mrs.

Centauri if he could say a few more words. She agreed, and he leaned into the microphone.

"Uh . . . I'm accepting this award in memory of my best friend. Neely Neubardt. He was smarter than I am. Maybe he would have won an award someday. Maybe he would have grown up to do something really great. But he got shot. So we'll never know. We all gotta do something so we don't lose more kids like Neely. 'Cause we are losing them. Every day. We gotta do something to stop it. *Now.*"

He felt Mrs. Centauri squeeze his hand. Langston stepped off the stage and sat back down with his parents. His mother kissed him on the cheek.

Most of the audience was in tears, even people who had never met Neely. The applause started quietly— then built to a roar.

· · · · ·

Back in thirteenth-century Rome the new pope opened the first of three books that had just arrived in a crate shipped from England. He glanced at the diagrams and notes.

"Hmmm . . . fascinating," he said to his aide. He examined the title on the book's cover. "*Opus Majus* . . . the world should know about this. Who did you say sent it?"

The aide pointed to the return address on the crate:

DR. ROGER BACON, OXFORD, ENGLAND.

. . . . .

In Mrs. Centauri's science class the next week the topic of study—entirely by coincidence, of course— happened to be Roger Bacon. Elliott Perkins, the class know-it-all, was pontificating as usual.

"Roger Bacon didn't invent anything!" Elliott said. "He just stole stuff from a lot of other scientists. And gunpowder! Look where *that* got us!"

Galvanized, Langston sprang from his chair. "That's not true! He was an original thinker. Which was really hard to be with that guy Jerome after him all the time! And gunpowder? Well, he knew it would do terrible things someday, and that worried him. A lot. I mean, it's not like the guy didn't have a heart. He rescued that crazy lady with the spiky hair from the asylum, he felt so bad when the pope died that he got trashed and sang 'Greensleeves.' He got kippers for Ptolemy—he even adopted Niles! It's just that Dr. Bacon thought that gunpowder might help the people of his own time and . . ."

Langston finally noticed that everyone was staring at him. *Uh-oh.*

"You know," Mrs. Centauri said, looking at him

suspiciously. "If I didn't know better, I'd almost say you knew the man. . . ."

"Uh . . . ," Langston said.

Just then a girl poked her head in the doorway.

"Come in! Sit down," Mrs. Centauri said cheerfully, spotting her. "Okay, you guys, I want you to meet our new student, Natalie. She's just moved here with her folks from New York. Don't make her feel like a space alien, okay?"

Langston couldn't take his eyes off this African-American girl. She looked exactly like . . .

"Hi," she said, smiling and sitting down at an empty desk next to Langston. She looked at him curiously. "Haven't I seen you someplace before?"

Langston was so stunned that all he could do was croak out, "Hi."

Shortly after, the school bell rang.

"Remember!" Mrs. Centauri said. "Quiz on Roger Bacon next week!"

The students gathered up their books and left the room.

Langston walked out with Natalie. He was so engrossed in talking to her that he didn't notice something had fallen out of his jacket pocket.

"Langston, you dropped your . . . ," Mrs. Centauri called after him, bending over to pick up the object. But he was already gone.

Mrs. Centauri looked closely at the silver coin in her palm. It looked brand new.

She read the date aloud: "1278."

Her eyes widened in astonishment, narrowed with suspicion—then certainty.

Mrs. Centauri ran to the door and shouted down the hall, "Langston Davis!!"

That night Langston visited the cemetery.

Moonlight glinted off the metal object he was smashing with a rock.

Langston placed the smashed gun on Neely's grave.

And he left it there.

෨෬෭

AUTHOR'S NOTE

I grew up in the 1960s, a time when all my heroes—President John F. Kennedy and his brother Senator Bobby Kennedy, the Reverend Martin Luther King Jr., and others—were being gunned down on what seemed an almost monthly basis, and as is true today, war overseas and gun violence on American soil were a constant. In those days schoolchildren and teens were not counseled by professionals as they are today when something terrible happens on the national scene, and most parents—so overwhelmed with shock and grief themselves by these tragic events—did not know how to speak to their children about them. Like many of my generation, I was traumatized by these killings and grew up with a passionate hatred of guns.

Each year in the United States nearly thirty thousand people are killed by guns (statistic from www.jointogether.org). I have often found myself thinking, *I wish guns had never been invented! Black Powder* grew out of that wish.

LINGUISTIC AND BIOGRAPHICAL NOTES

Had you lived in England in the time of Roger Bacon[1] (ca.1214–ca.1292), you would have found people speaking a language called Middle English that would make about as much sense to you as Greek. (I'm assuming you don't speak Greek.) And, when teaching, writing, or speaking with other friars, Roger Bacon would have used another old language that you may not understand either: Latin. So I've used my own language for this book. The medieval epithets used by the cranky Bacon, however ("You beslubbering, beef-witted barnacle!" etc.), are actual curses used during the Middle Ages, though probably not till later than 1278.

As for the Yiddish used in this story—the language spoken by the thirteenth-century milk wagon driver, Rosenbloom—it is indeed a real language that developed among European Jews during medieval times from a combination of Jewish-French and Jewish-Italian dialects, and later included elements of German and Slavic as well. The original languages of the Jews were Hebrew and Aramaic (which are two ingredients of Yiddish), and Hebrew is still spoken today.

---

1. Roger Bacon was not really a doctor; he was referred to by the honorary title or nickname "Doctor Mirabilis" ("wonderful teacher") only after his death. And even though some Franciscan friars are also ordained priests, Roger Bacon was not. He only took what is known as "minor orders" to become a Franciscan. In those long-ago days had Friar Roger Bacon also been ordained as a priest he would indeed have been called "Father Bacon" (as he angrily insists to the clumsy visiting professor at Oxford) and not "Brother Roger."

In my story, I chose to make Friar Bacon a priest so he could give absolution while taking confessions and do other priestly duties. And I wanted Niles to call him "Father" from the start, to underline their evolving father-son–like relationship.

Many American Jews, including my own parents (who were born in the United States, the children of European immigrants), speak a little Yiddish, and many Yiddishisms—such as *klutz, ersatz,* and various forms of *meshuggener*—have entered the English language, especially in places like New York City, which has a large Jewish population. One hundred years ago about 90 percent of the Jews in Europe were able to speak Yiddish. Today the language is less commonly spoken, especially among younger Jews, though some of them are learning the language by taking courses, to keep it alive. According to a recent article in the *New York Post,* more than one hundred thousand New Yorkers can speak Yiddish. Seven subway stations in the borough of Brooklyn (an area of New York City with a substantial number of traditional Jews) now have ticket vending machines that offer instructions in Yiddish. And in 2004 a new translation of American children's author Dr. Seuss's *The Cat in the Hat* was published in Yiddish (*Di Kats der Payats*).

Star Trek fans will notice that the Klingon language in this story is accurate.

Bacon was indeed a scientific genius way ahead of his time. He believed the earth was round more than two hundred years before Ferdinand Magellan proved this by circumnavigating the globe. He was the first scientist to think up the idea of the telescope ("For we can so shape transparent bodies," Bacon wrote, "and arrange them in such a way with respect to our sight and objects of vision, that the rays will be reflected and bent in any direction we desire, and under any angle we wish, we may see the object near or at a distance. . . . So we might also cause the Sun, Moon and stars in appearance to descend here below"), the automobile ("Cars can be made so that without animals they will move with unbelievable rapidity"), and the airplane. And he invented reading spectacles. A crater of the moon has been named Bacon in his honor.

To expand his knowledge, Bacon—who became a Franciscan friar at the age of thirty-three—studied ancient texts written in Greek and Arabic. But many in the church at the time believed it was wrong to study non-Christian philosophers and that the only way toward knowledge was to study the Scriptures. So Bacon had many enemies in the church leadership.

Roger Bacon taught at Oxford University for many years, though he was no longer teaching there in 1278, when my story takes place. After becoming a Franciscan, Bacon discontinued teaching at Oxford but continued his scientific research there.[2]

In 1256, when Richard of Cornwall took over as head of the academic section of Bacon's Franciscan order, Bacon was forbidden to continue his studies and experiments at Oxford and was sent to a monastery in Paris, France.

"They forced me with unspeakable violence to obey their will," Bacon wrote.

Other than by writing letters, Bacon had no contact with the outside world for the next ten years. He was permitted

2. By the way, if you are wondering why, in my story, Friar Bacon lived in a house rather than in the Oxford friary with the rest of his Franciscan brothers, my convenient but entirely fictional answer is that one of his science experiments blew up their cellar, so they banished him.

to teach math but was forbidden to conduct his scientific experiments.

Bacon did work on a three-volume encyclopedia of all knowledge with Pope Clement IV's support. This is how it came about:

In 1264 Bacon wrote to Cardinal Foulques proposing that he write a science book (which turned out to be the encyclopedia) to benefit the church. The cardinal, who became Pope Clement IV in the following year, misunderstood at first and thought Bacon had *already* written his encyclopedia. When Bacon explained that it hadn't been written yet, the pope urged him to go ahead with his plan—but told him to write the books in secret, since Bacon's research went against the rules of his Franciscan order.

When Bacon was finished writing the first volume, he had his favorite student, John, carry it to the pope in Rome. But Pope Clement IV died before he could read the book. After the pope's death in 1268 (there's no evidence he was poisoned) Bacon's dreams of finishing his encyclopedia died too.

Bacon continued to be persecuted by his fellow Franciscans. Around the year 1278 they sent him to prison in Italy for teaching his dangerous, heretical ideas (what they called "suspected sorcery"). Bacon—and other friars whose beliefs differed from their Franciscan superiors'—was imprisoned at Ancona, where he was kept in solitary confinement and was not even permitted to speak to his prison guards. His imprisonment probably lasted at least twelve years. Bacon was finally released after a new, more compassionate leader, Raymond

Gaufredi, took charge of his Franciscan order and set all the prisoners of Ancona free.

Jerome of Ascoli was a real person, the minister general of Bacon's Franciscan order, who eventually (in 1288) became Pope Nicholas IV. He was not, however, the devil himself. Some historians say that Jerome was responsible for imprisoning Bacon for his "dangerous novelties" and "suspected sorcery." Others dispute whether Bacon was ever imprisoned at all and claim that even if he was, the reasons for this had to do with his theological beliefs rather than his scientific theories.

Roger Bacon's final written work was a condemnation of corrupt elements within the Christian Church. It was published a year after his death.

Some of the information about Roger Bacon mentioned in the preceeding paragraphs was acquired by reading a biographical article about him by J. J. O'Connor and E. F. Robertson, available online at http://www-gap.dcs .st-and.ac.uk/~history/Mathematicians/Bacon.html. A recent biography in book form is *The First Scientist: A Life of Roger Bacon* by Brian Clegg (Carroll and Graf, 2003).

BACON'S "DISCOVERY" OF GUNPOWDER

Sometime during the mid-1200s, Roger Bacon developed the formula for gunpowder that would make possible the invention of guns several decades later.

According to most historians, Bacon didn't really invent gunpowder; he may have just rediscovered and improved the formula for gunpowder created much earlier by the Chinese. He spoke fluent Arabic, so it's also possible Bacon could have learned about gunpowder from a nomadic tribe of Arab tradesmen, the Saracens, who shuttled between Asia and Europe. Or he could have seen Chinese or Indian documents that explained the formula.

In his recent book, *Gunpowder,* author Jack Kelly acknowledges that Roger Bacon was the first European to write of gunpowder, but Kelly claims that Bacon's formula is only "the stuff of legend" because it "cannot definitely be attributed to Bacon, and the coded 'formula' is open to any number of interpretations."[3]

But other historians believe that Bacon himself invented gunpowder—through his own experimentation—even though by that time the Chinese had been using a less concentrated form of this explosive for years. News of the Chinese version of gunpowder (first recorded in a book in 1044) didn't officially reach Europe till years after Bacon's discovery, when Marco Polo returned to Italy with stories of this remarkable substance.

Bacon's formula for black powder, or gunpowder—six parts (or seven, depending on how it's interpreted) saltpeter ("the petral stone"), five parts "young willow" charcoal, five parts sulfur[4]—was written in a secret anagrammatic code. So he must

3. Jack Kelly, *Gunpowder: Alchemy, Bombards, and Pyrotechnics: The History of the Explosive that Changed the World.* (New York: Basic Books, 2004), 25.

4. Science writer and Roger Bacon biographer Brian Clegg tells me: "Bacon's formula for gunpowder wasn't very good! There was too little saltpeter in it, which meant his version was only suitable for creating loud noises, smoke, and flashes to scare the enemy (which is how he suggested it could be used)." This formula first appeared in Roger Bacon's letter "Concerning the Marvelous Power of Art and Nature and Concerning the Nullity of Magic."

have known that it could be dangerous if it got into the wrong hands. Indeed, as early as 1267 he warned that although gunpowder had till then been only "a child's toy" (in the form of firecrackers), in the future it could have far more serious consequences: "By the flash and combustion of fires, and by the horror of the sounds, wonders can be wrought, and at any distance that we wish, so that a man can hardly protect himself or endure it." It's possible that Bacon's formula for gunpowder remained a secret till around 1910, when a British army colonel decoded it. But by then, of course, guns and gunpowder had already been in use for hundreds of years.

No one knows for sure when guns were invented or by whom. Some sources say that early, primitive guns were a Chinese invention in the late 1200s. Others say that the earliest guns were developed by Arabs and first appeared in the country now known as Morocco around the year 1300. Most scholars agree that the Chinese originated bamboo cannonlike firearms long before metal guns were invented.

Roger Bacon could not have foreseen the full extent of the negative impact that his "discovery" of gunpowder would have on the world. He deserves to be remembered for his scientific genius, his creative spirit, and his indomitable courage in speaking out for his beliefs—despite all those who sought to extinguish the brilliant light he brought to the darkness of the Middle Ages.

HISTORICAL, SCIENTIFIC, AND GEOGRAPHICAL NOTES

In my story I moved the moment of Bacon's discovery of gunpowder from the mid-1200s to January 1278 to coincide with the year of his actual imprisonment—by Jerome of Ascoli—though Bacon was really held in an Italian convent, not a Parisian jail.

The geographic distances implied in *Black Powder* are fanciful. In the thirteenth century it would not have been possible to travel from England to Scotland, or from Calais to Paris, in less than a day. I compressed the amount of time required to travel these distances to keep the story moving along.

The magnetic compass was not invented by Roger Bacon, as my story implies, but by the Chinese, probably as early as the Qin dynasty (221–206 B.C.). The earliest compasses used spoon-shaped lodestones (a type of iron ore containing the mineral magnetite, which has magnetic properties and north-south polarity) and were used only as pointers for Chinese fortune-telling boards. These bronze diviner's boards were believed to predict the future or help determine the best place and time for scheduling important events. To see a photograph of this early compass, go to the Web site of Smith College's Museum of Ancient Inventions: www.smith.edu /hsc/museum/ancient_inventions/compass2.html.

By the eighth century compasses used magnetized needles instead of lodestones as direction pointers. In the next two centuries compasses became common as navigational aids on Chinese ships. Magnetized needles point north (toward magnetic north, more loosely called the North Pole) because they are drawn toward the natural pull of the earth's magnetic field. But if you were standing directly over the North or South Pole, the compass would spin freely because from the North Pole there is no north, and from the South Pole every direction is north.

Clocks and watches as we know them today did not exist in 1278. The first mechanical clocks began to appear on public buildings in Italy in the 1300s, and the first portable timepiece was invented in 1504 by Peter Henlein in Nuremburg, Germany. Pocket sundials existed by the tenth century.

The famous clock on Oxford's Carfax Tower (near which Langston finds Mr. Rosenbloom's house)—the tower being all that remains of Saint Martin's Church, originally built in Bacon's era, then demolished twice and rebuilt in the 1800s—had two mechanical figures, called quarterboys, that hammered out each quarter hour on bells. You can see a copy of the original clock at Oxford's Carfax Tower today— though I've heard a rumor that the quarterboys can no longer do their job and that tourists sometimes stand there waiting in vain for the clock to strike. Legend has it that occasionally townsfolk used to stand in the tower and throw coins, stones, and arrows at the Oxford students walking below, so after 1340 the university shortened the tower by twenty feet (it's now seventy-four feet tall).

The calendar system in use in England and America changed at least twice between Bacon's era and our own. For example, in 1752, when Britain and its American colonies switched from the Julian calendar to the Gregorian calendar, George Washington's birthday (he was born in 1731) suddenly "changed" from February 11 to February 22. In addition, there is an eight-hour time difference between California and England (when it's morning in Oxford, it's still nighttime in Los Angeles), which obviously existed as a physical reality even before time zones were invented. To avoid confusing readers, I did not take into account any of these factors when calculating dates and times for various locations in my story, or when moving Langston from one place or century to another.

Construction work on the exterior of the U.S. Capitol dome was completed in December 1863, when the final sections (head and shoulders) of the nineteen-foot bronze statue of a woman, called *Freedom*, was lifted into place on top of it. Internal work on the dome continued, however, till January 1866, when the scaffolding was finally removed from under Constantino Brumidi's fresco *The Apotheosis of Washington* 180 feet above the Rotunda floor. For the sake of my story, I postponed completion of external work on the dome till April 1865 so Langston could witness construction still in progress.

One medical note: Langston flips upside down in space, hoping this will "get more blood to his brain." But in reality the weightlessness of space tends to make fluids in the blood vessels rise toward the head, since there is no gravity to hold them down. That's why space shuttle astronauts' faces look puffy when they're on a voyage.

It should also be noted that the old Pioneer spacecraft that Langston sees during his journey through the cosmos is really out there, but it doesn't have any name or number engraved on its hull, and it is called "Pioneer Ten," not "Pioneer X."

INFORMATION ABOUT GUN VIOLENCE IN AMERICA

A July 21, 2004, article by Kevin Johnson in *USA Today* reports that after nearly a decade of decline in the 1990s, gang violence is resurging in the twenty-first century— especially in smaller American cities and suburbs. The increase is being attributed to the recent release of senior gang members from jails, as well as diversion of police resources from fighting crime to fighting international terrorism. Law enforcement officials in southern California estimate that nearly one in every one hundred residents of Los Angeles County belongs to a gang.

In 1998, gunshot wounds were the leading cause of death for African-American males aged fifteen to thirty-four, and second only to car crashes as the most common cause of injury or death in the U.S. for young people of all races aged ten to twenty-four (see www.bradycampaign.org). As reported by Johnson, gun-related homicides in the U.S. jumped 50 percent between 1999 and 2002, according to a study commissioned by a coalition of police chiefs, called Fight Crime: Invest in Kids. In response to the growing problem, in July 2004 the House of Representatives voted to establish the National Gang Intelligence Center, which, if also approved by the Senate, would help law enforcement officials track gang members who commit crimes. That same summer the Million Mom March demonstrated in many American cities to urge Congress to renew the Assault Weapons Ban, a law enacted in 1994 that Congress allowed to expire on September 13, 2004.

Following are recent figures from the Centers for Disease Control and Prevention's National Center for Health Statistics (as reported on the Web site www.kidsandguns.org):[5]

- Between 1996 and 2001, 2,836 American children and teens were murdered using guns.

- In 2002, 13,053 kids under the age of twenty were injured by firearms, and another 16,082 by BB guns or pellet guns.

- Between 1992 and 2001, 1,273 children and teens used guns to commit suicide.

- The rate of firearms-related death in the U.S. among children under the age of fifteen is nearly a dozen times higher than it is in twenty-five other industrialized nations combined.

5. Centers for Disease Control and Prevention, National Center for Health Statistics, *National Vital Statistics Report,* vol. 52, no. 3, *Deaths: Final Data for 2001,* (PHS) 2003-1120 (Washington, D.C., 2003).

- In 2001 a child or teen was killed in a firearms-related accident or suicide every eight hours. The toll for 2002 increased to 2,867 dead—one death nearly every three hours.

Here are some other facts regarding guns in America:

- Forty-seven percent of high school students (60 percent of boys) said they could obtain a gun if they wanted to, 22 percent of middle school students (31 percent of boys) said they could get a firearm.[6]

- Thirty-eight percent of households in the U.S. have at least one gun and 24 percent contain a handgun.[7]

- A 2002 study reported that 5.7 percent of high school students reported carrying a gun more than once in the previous thirty days. Male students (10.3 percent) were significantly more likely than females (1.3 percent) to have carried a gun.[8]

6. Josephson Institute of Ethics, *2000 Report Card: The Ethics of American Youth* (Los Angeles, April 2001).

7. Johns Hopkins Center for Gun Policy and Research, National Opinion Research Center, *Fall 1998 National Gun Policy Survey: Questionnaire with Unweighted Frequencies and Weighted Percentages* (Baltimore, Md., 1998).

8. Centers for Disease Control and Prevention, *Morbidity and Mortality Weekly Report*, vol. 51, no. SS-4, "Youth Risk Behavior Surveillance—United States, 2001" (Atlanta, 2002).

In addition to school shootings that make the national news—such as the 1999 Columbine High massacre in Littleton, Colorado, and the Red Lake, Minnesota, killings in 2005—there are many other incidents of gun violence at schools each year. Columbine was one of a dozen shootings in American schools—from Alaska to Georgia—in an eighteen-month period (CNN and www.keystosaferschools.com).

How to Get Involved in Preventing Gun Violence in Your Community

Kids and teens, parents and teachers, who want to learn more about this subject can find helpful information by going to the following Web sites:

Common Sense About Kids and Guns
www.kidsandguns.org

The Brady Campaign to Prevent Gun Violence United
with the Million Mom March
www.bradycampaign.org
www.millionmommarch.org

The Brady Center to Prevent Gun Violence
www.bradycenter.org

The Coalition to Stop Gun Violence and The
Educational Fund to Stop Gun Violence
http://action.csgv.org

25¢